"Kitchens always have this romantic effect on me."

"Keep away from me, or I'll bop you on the head with Aunt Edna's rolling pin."

"Wouldn't you like to be kissed in the kitchen?" he teased.

"No."

"Are you sure? I'm a terrific kisser."

He knows he can raise my blood pressure just by dropping his voice an octave, and he's absolutely enjoying it, Chris decided. She pushed against his chest with both hands, hoping he wouldn't feel her heart pounding in her chest. "You're horrid."

"I like when your voice gets all husky and tremulous like that." His cobalt eyes lowered as he played with the zipper on her sweat suit jacket. "There's a nice chemistry between us. You knew it as soon as I did— when we looked at each other under the hood of your car. For some reason it scares the heck out of you."

"I don't want to get involved."

"I know that. That's why I'm moving in..."

Steffie Hall

Steffie Hall was born in New Jersey and has a degree in Fine Arts. Although her teens and twenties were spent as a serious painter, and her thirties were consumed by motherhood, now that she's in her forties, she once again feels the need to extend herself, and has taken up writing.

Her days start at five o'clock in the morning, when she stumbles out to the car to ferry her fourteen-year-old aspiring Olympian daughter to the skating rink. At seven-thirty, she sends her sixteen-year-old bona fide genius son to school. Somewhere in between, her husband leaves for the university where he teaches mathematics. At seven thirty-five, she feeds her five birds, a rabbit, a cat, and two dogs. It's at approximately eight o'clock that she finally "slices into the fillet of her day." Says Steffie, "Ensconced behind a blinking computer screen, surrounded by my favorite photographs, under the domination of a bright yellow clock and a frantic orange calendar, I get to write stories. I especially like creating characters like HERO AT LARGE's Aunt Edna, who might be bothersome or unattractive in real life, and presenting them to the reader in such a way that she must be tolerant of them and find them enjoyable."

Dear Reader:

For May, we're pleased to offer you a spring bouquet of quality romances, some emphasizing lightness and laughter, others highlighting suspense and high drama ... and each one revealing how absolutely wondrous love can be the second time around.

Pat Dalton combines humor and intrigue in her inimitable fashion in *Conspiracy of Hearts* (#406). "John" and "Eric" are merely two of this hero's aliases—he's a spy who seeks to come in from the cold and find a safe, steady job with the help of employment counselor Lisa Rollins. Instead, he and Lisa find themselves on the lam, pursued by both the bad guys *and* the good guys! "John-Eric" gives Lisa a crash course in espionage techniques ... while *he* learns some amazing lessons about love. Fans of *Remington Steele* and *Moonlighting* will cherish this one.

If your taste runs to romantic adventure reminiscent of *Romancing the Stone*, don't miss Lee Williams's thirteenth Second Chance at Love novel, *Heat Wave* (#407). Lee's personal knowledge of the movie business is a definite bonus in this tale that unites film-location scout Nadine McGuane and sexy anthropologist Zack Matthews in a sensual South American locale. Nadine's less than enthralled by heat, hurricanes, bloodthirsty mosquitoes ... and the prospect of sharing a hut with dashing, disturbing Zack. An erotic chemistry too powerful to be denied builds between them, proving once again that love will find a way, even in the heart of the jungle.

Courtney Ryan has been cited by reviewer Melinda Helfer as epitomizing "that special blend of humor and romance that is Second Chance at its best" (*Romantic Times*, vol. 34, Dec./Jan.), and readers of *Temporary Angel* (#408) will agree. As a teenager, Ashley Evans was Grantville's resident Good Girl—now she's nationally notorious as the cover girl on a waterproof poster that men hang in the shower! Ashley resents being labeled, whether angel or sinner, and it seems only her gorgeous, platonic male roommate, musician Jesse Stark, can offer her detached understanding. But Jesse's head over heels in love with this complex woman, and he pursues Ashley from L.A. to Grantville and back again, until he captures her heart and her hand.

In *Hero at Large* (#409), Steffie Hall debuts with a memorable, daffy domestic comedy. When skating coach Chris Nelson's car breaks down, her unlikely white knight to the rescue is carpenter Ken Callahan. Ken's raw male magnetism unnerves Chris to the point where she inadvertently breaks his arm. And later that day, Ken turns up—like Goldilocks—sleeping in Chris's bed! A nervous thrill of anticipation warns her of the passionate trouble to come ... Here's a vintage comedy of errors scintillating with banter from an outstanding new author.

Carole Buck must be on everyone's list of all-time favorite romance authors, and in *Chasing Rainbows* (#410), she brings her soufflé-light wit to the world of torts and mergers. Laura Newton, a paralegal at a prestigious Boston law firm, has sworn off noble causes since her divorce from an overzealous activist—until she falls like a ton of bricks for one Kenyon C. Sutton, a.k.a. Casey the Crusader. A public interest lawyer, Casey intervenes when Laura's mother is unexpectedly arrested for disturbing the peace ... and he, in turn, disturbs Laura's peace of mind as they chase— and ultimately capture—rainbows in the corridors of Old Money politics and power. Not since Perry Mason has the law made for such entertaining reading.

An exotic clime and a clash of wills cause tempers—and passions—to run hot in Cass McAndrew's *Primitive Glory* (#411). When Amanda Lacey is sent to the Himalayas to whip field agronomist Eric Nichols into shape, she's totally unprepared for the most trying—and sensually disturbing—man she's ever met. Brilliant at work, devastatingly handsome, Eric's too stubborn to follow home-office rules ... but he pursues Amanda with ardent determination. New author Cass McAndrew joins these vividly depicted, strong-willed characters with breathtaking landscapes and breath-catching action to create an explosive and steamy love story.

Happy reading!

Joan Marlow

Joan Marlow, Editor
SECOND CHANCE AT LOVE
The Berkley Publishing Group
200 Madison Avenue
New York, NY 10016

SECOND CHANCE AT LOVE

STEFFIE HALL
HERO AT LARGE

A
SECOND CHANCE AT LOVE
BOOK

**To Mom, Dad, Pete, Alex, and Peter
—thanks for everything**

HERO AT LARGE

Copyright © 1987 by Steffie Hall

First edition published May 1987

First printing

"Second Chance at Love" and the butterfly emblem are trademarks belonging to Jove Publications, Inc.

Printed in the United States of America

Second Chance at Love books are published by
The Berkley Publishing Group
200 Madison Avenue, New York, NY 10016.

Chapter One

CHRIS NELSON MUTTERED an indiscernible oath and expelled a cloud of frost into the bone-chilling early-morning air. Even in the inky predawn blackness, it was clear that a new splotch of oil had mysteriously grown beneath her battered tan hatchback during the night. She plunged her key into the lock and wrenched the dented, rusting door open, then slid behind the wheel and tried the ignition. Nothing.

"Just start one more time, and tomorrow I'll get you fixed," she pledged, knowing full well that it was an empty promise. She didn't believe in getting cars fixed—she felt too hopelessly intimidated by car mechanics. As a world-class athlete she'd conducted media interviews with the aplomb of a seasoned celebrity. She'd displayed good-humored optimism as a runner-up and honest satisfaction as a winner, and earned a worldwide reputation for her feisty personality and quick wit under pressure. But she knew in her heart of hearts that while she could hold her own with the president of the United States, she would never be a match for a man holding an air wrench. She cringed at the memory of her last experience, when she'd paid an exorbitant amount to fix a glamus—while meekly suspecting that no such part existed.

No, she decided, keeping her thoughts silent—and thus

secret from the car—it was much more sensible simply to drive the dying machine into the ground, walk away from it with whatever dignity she could muster, and buy a new one. She gingerly tried the ignition one more time and almost cheered out loud when it caught. She pulled away from her Fairfax, Virginia, town house with a glorious feeling of victory, closing her eyes to the red light flashing on the dashboard. Dismissing the clouds of gray smoke as condensation, she bravely eased the sputtering car onto the highway.

Ten minutes later when she stopped for a red light on the Little River Turnpike, the car shuddered, belched an acrid blast of opaque exhaust, and stalled out. Chris felt her heart drop to her stomach. "Please," she whispered, wrapping her fingers gently around the steering wheel, "tell me you're not ready for the big junkyard in the sky." She narrowed her eyes and patted the dashboard. "I'll let you rest a minute, and then we'll try it again." The light changed. Traffic rushed past in the November gloom: Northern Virginia was en route to the Pentagon and downtown D.C. Chris held her breath and tried again. Silence.

"Dammit." She peered into her rearview mirror at headlights waiting patiently behind her. Throwing her hands up in frustration, she punched the button that turned on the emergency flashers. The lights shining into her back window were high. Probably a truck. That was good—men who drove trucks always knew a lot about car engines, she reasoned. She watched hopefully as the driver emerged and strode toward her, then shifted her gaze to the flashing red light she'd so easily ignored only minutes ago.

Knuckles rapped on Chris's side window. "Got a problem?"

Chris's eyes stayed glued to the warning light on her dash. "It just suddenly stopped. I think it might have something to do with this little red light."

"Why don't you try to kick it over one more time."

She turned the key and listened morosely to the churning motor.

"Stop."

"Only thing in decent working order on this whole crummy car is the stupid warning light," Chris muttered through gritted teeth. Her peripheral vision registered a shift of weight, and she felt rather than saw the grin of good-humored masculine resignation.

"Maybe we should push it over to the shoulder, and I'll take a look under the hood."

Several minutes later, Chris stomped her feet in the cold as she watched him poke around at the engine. He was very tall—maybe six-two, she guessed—and nicely put together. He wore scuffed, waffle-soled construction worker's boots and well-washed jeans that clung suggestively to long, muscular legs. A faded navy blue hooded sweat shirt draped comfortably over broad shoulders. A smudged tan down vest hung unbuttoned over the sweat shirt.

He flicked a flashlight beam over rubber tubing and fan belt, his black hair falling in unkempt waves over his eyes. A heavy beard made his dark skin look villainously swarthy, and the tousled hair curled over his ears and halfway down his neck. He made an attempt to brush it back onto his forehead and noticed Chris watching him. "I need a haircut," he explained, flashing a boyish grin that displayed perfect white teeth.

Chris felt her heart tumble unexpectedly at his disarming smile and immediately an image of Little Red Riding Hood and the big bad wolf popped into her head. What a ridiculous thing to think of—yet there was definitely a predatory air about him. Wolfish, in an attractive sort of way, she decided. And incredibly handsome ... but a slob. Probably on his way to pour a foundation or dig a septic system.

Determined to prove herself invulnerable to his charms, she leaned on the front quarter panel and stuck her head under the hood with him. "Well?" she asked expectantly, "what do you think?"

"For starters ... there's not a drop of oil in it."

Chris looked up and found herself staring into magnetic blue-black eyes made even more compelling by thick curling lashes and crinkly smile lines that testified to an active, outdoor life and a generous sense of humor. She watched dry-mouthed as he directed his flashlight to the riot of yellow-orange curls that surrounded her perfectly oval face. His inspection traveled from her almond-shaped hazel eyes, down to her small pixie nose and her bow-shaped mouth that shone with just a touch of pink lip-slicker. She licked her lips and answered in a voice that suddenly sounded strangely husky, "Is that bad?"

The look of incredulity that fluttered across his eyes was replaced immediately with a gently mocking curiosity. He played the light over her ringless hands. "I think you need a new man in your life." The timbre of his voice lowered. "Someone who takes better care of your . . . mechanical needs?"

Chris rolled her eyes. She was late for work, her car had just succumbed to terminal neglect, and her feet were freezing. She was in no mood to field a double entendre from a scruffy stranger . . . even if he did make her heart skip a few beats. She stood abruptly, hitting her head on the inside of the hood. There was a loud *spronnng*, and Chris jumped away just in time to see the hood come crashing down on two long, sweat shirt–clad arms.

His breath hissed from between clenched teeth. He swore softly, resting his forehead on the cool metal of the car. "Nice work, lady," he rasped. "Do you always cripple men who stop to help you? Or am I special?"

Chris opened her eyes wide in horror. "I'm sorry—it was an accident!"

"Uh-huh."

Chris glared at him. "Well, you shouldn't be making passes at women you stop to help. It's like Sir Walter Raleigh carrying some grateful lady over a mud puddle and then trying to sneak a look under her skirt when he sets her down. This was a well-deserved accident. An act of God," she tagged on for dramatic effect.

He nodded his head in mute agreement. Beads of sweat had begun to appear at his hairline. "Do you suppose God would mind if you got the damn hood off my arms?"

"Sorry." She held the hood while he awkwardly started to move his arms. He flexed one gingerly, then winced when he tried to raise the other. Chris Nelson was the sort of person who rescued baby birds and felt guilty about stepping on ants. She cried when people were hurt on television, and sent money to aid starving Africans, but she found it difficult to muster any sympathy for the man standing in front of her. He was so big and capable looking, and so aggressive. He was so roguishly shabby. And he silently emanated a casually checked sexuality that she suspected could knock her socks off if she gave it half a chance.

Standing to his full, imposing height, he cradled his left arm tenderly against his body. "My right arm seems to be okay, but the left is definitely broken." His voice was quiet, calm. "Is there a hospital near here?"

"There are two hospitals in the area—both about ten minutes away. Maybe a little longer in morning traffic."

He looked at her expectantly. "Well?"

"Well, what?"

"Lady, you just broke my arm. Aren't you at least going to offer to drive me to the hospital?"

Chris looked at him tentatively, her lip caught between her teeth, while she debated the danger of being alone in a car with him.

"For Pete's sake, I'm not going to attack you. I've got a broken arm."

"You look disreputable."

His gaze drifted down over himself in amazement. "I suppose you're right." He tipped his head back and laughed softly. "I've been called lots of things, but you're the first person in a long time to tell me I'm disreputable looking." He motioned to his truck. "I hate to be pushy, but my arm is killing me, and I can't shift my truck with a broken arm. Since you're the cause of this disaster, I think the least you can do is drive me to a doctor."

He was right, she thought dismally. "Okay. I'll take you to the hospital." She shook her finger at him in warning. "So help me . . . if you make one false move I'll drive you straight to the state police."

His gaze swept slowly over her, assessing her, and Chris felt suddenly unaccountably flustered—self-conscious of her tousled curls, her slim, athletic body bundled in her gray running suit and bright red vest. "You're not a minor, are you?"

Chris pulled a large athletic bag from the back seat of her car and locked it. "I'm twenty-nine, and if you tell me I look like Little Orphan Annie I might break your other arm."

"There is a resemblance."

"Don't push it." She stood facing his truck. It was one of those little teeny foreign things made to look sporty with wide striping on the side and fancy wheels—and it seemed to be in perfect condition. Sure, it's easy for him, she thought grimly. He probably knows if it has a glamus. A huge black dog sat behind the wheel. Chris looked at the man beside her. "There's a dog in there."

"Yeah."

"That's the second-biggest dog I've ever seen."

"It's a Rottweiler."

"It must weigh two hundred pounds. We won't all fit."

"Of course we will. This truck seats three."

"This truck would have to have rubber doors to seat three."

He swung himself into the truck and settled beside the panting Rottweiler. "Come on," he coaxed. "He's a good dog. See? He's smiling. He likes you."

Chris set her bag on the floor between his feet and trudged around to the driver's side. "Why me?" she groaned. "Why do these things always happen to me?" She opened the driver's side door and slid in next to the mountain of dog, trying politely to nudge him over. He didn't move. He draped his huge head on her shoulder and drooled down the front of her red vest. Chris rolled her eyes in disgust. "Oh for goodness' sake. Hey, you!" she called between the dog's ears. "What's your name?"

There was a brief hesitation. "Ken Callahan."

"Ken Callahan, I can't drive with your dog drooling on me."

He sighed. "Okay."

The passenger door opened and slammed shut. Chris watched Ken Callahan jog around the truck. Not her type, she told herself, but she had to admire his style. Even with a broken arm, he moved with the fluid ease of an athlete. He opened the door and jerked his thumb at Chris in an obvious order. "Out!" Maneuvering his large frame behind the wheel, he used his good arm to shove the dog clear to the window. He settled himself next to the Rottweiler and straddled the gearshift. "Is this better?"

"Do you drool?"

"Another ten minutes with you, and I'm going to be drooling and babbling and committing mayhem."

Chris slid behind the wheel again and found herself pressed thigh to thigh with Ken Callahan. There wasn't an inch to spare between the dog and the man. And the gearshift was hopelessly lost from sight between Ken Callahan's legs. *I should have left well enough alone*—she grimaced—*I was better off with the Rottweiler.*

"Um . . . Ken?"—she tried to shift in her seat—"We don't all fit in this truck."

"If I'd known you were going to break my arm, I would have left my dog at home." His voice was rapidly losing its calm modulation.

Wriggling again, Chris shot him a black look. "Don't get cranky. For two cents I'd leave you stranded here."

"I'd give you the two cents, but I can't get into my pocket with my broken arm."

Chris narrowed her eyes and counted to ten. "Can't he ride in back?"

"He'll jump out—and please don't suggest that *I* ride in back . . . it's starting to rain."

Chris squinted miserably at the windshield. He was right. It was raining. "Fine," she said through clenched teeth, "just keep out of my way." Ken Callahan made a fruitless attempt to move his long legs while she turned the key in the ignition. She switched the lights on, but the interior was barely lit by the glowing dashboard. Pressing her lips tightly together, she reached between his legs in search of the gearshift.

There was a sharp intake of breath, and the man squirmed beside her. "Lady, if you'll just tell me what it is you're looking for . . . I'll be glad to help you find it."

She swallowed and willed her voice not to quaver. "I'm looking for the gearshift."

He took her hand and placed it on the plastic knob. "Maybe you could be careful when you put this thing into first? This is a little cramped quarters."

She eased the stick back into gear and felt her thumb brush against the inside of his thigh. She closed her eyes in disbelief and scorching embarrassment. "This is impossible! Can't you scrinch into the seat a little?"

"I'm scrinched as much as I can scrinch. If you'd just get moving, you could put it into second, and we'd all feel better."

Chris spun the wheels and peeled out into the stream of traffic.

Ken Callahan gripped the dashboard. "Holy cow, now I know how you got all those dents in your car."

"Do you want to drive?"

"You wouldn't want to know what I'd like to do," he returned between clenched teeth.

Chris clutched the wheel with all the desperation of a drowning woman clinging to a leaking life preserver. She couldn't ever remember feeling so disturbed by a man. Every move she made pressed against hard muscle and sent suspicious sensations fluttering along her nerve endings, resulting in an odd mixture of fear, annoyance, and raw physical attraction. She focused her attention on the road and took a deep breath to steady herself. It was a ridiculous situation, and she knew it was going to get worse before it got better. She was up to fifty miles an hour and still driving in third gear. The motor whined in protest. She had to put the truck into fourth gear, but that meant sliding her hand along the inside of his right leg, again. *This is my punishment for neglecting my car,* she agonized. *I didn't feed it oil, and I lied to it, and the Car Fairy is getting even.*

Ken Callahan cleared his throat nervously. "Uh, you really should put it into fourth."

"I know that." She glanced at him in the rearview mirror and realized he was biting back laughter. "Something funny?"

"You're kinda cute when you're all flustered."

She made a grunting sound of pure annoyance. The only thing worse than being flustered was having him know she was flustered. She wrapped her fist around the gearshift and plunged it back with a vengeance.

"Yeow!" he gasped, jumping out of the way and smashing the surprised dog against the car door. "Watch what you're doing with that thing. I hope to have children some day."

"If you make me any more nervous you're not going to live to have breakfast . . . much less children."

He settled into his seat, and Chris felt his eyes watching her speculatively. Embarrassment, and some other emotion she didn't care to analyze, rose in fiery waves clear to the roots of her hair.

He touched her flaming cheek with the back of his hand. "You're blushing."

She groaned inwardly. Blushing was an understatement. If her face got any hotter, she'd be able to fry an egg on her forehead.

"This is a first for me. I've never been able to make a woman blush. I didn't think modern women did that sort of thing." He wound his finger around an orange curl and tugged lightly. "It's nice." His voice was soft and low. It reminded Chris of fine brandy that had the unusual ability to simultaneously soothe and stimulate. "What's your name?"

"Chris Nelson."

"That's a very no-nonsense name for a slightly crazy lady. You look more like a Tootsie or a Fanny . . . or maybe a Lucy."

"Lucy is my daughter's name."

"You have a daughter?" There was a moment of pregnant silence while he digested the fact of her motherhood. "How old is she?"

"Seven."

"And her father?"

"Gone."

"Poor man. Life must always seem dull after living with you."

She gave him a sidewise glance and saw a smile threatening to emerge at the corners of his mouth. Damn him. He was laughing at her again. How dare he enjoy himself when she was so uncomfortable. And he didn't even have the good grace to be obnoxious—the rat was downright adorable.

He shifted his broken arm, trying to find a more comfortable position. "Is it much farther?"

"The hospital turnoff is just ahead. Does your arm hurt?"

"It's down to a dull throb."

Chris had an insane urge to kiss his arm and make it better. Maternal instincts, she assured herself. Nothing more than a hormone imbalance left over from childbirth. The fact that he was incredibly handsome had nothing to do with it.

They were traveling down a four-lane highway with a safety island running down the middle. Chris pulled into the left-turn lane, stopped at the intersection, and watched the oncoming traffic. Rain pelted the windshield, making it difficult to see openings in the morning rush of commuters.

"Here we are," Chris announced, finally able to complete the turn. She pulled the truck into the brightly lit parking lot and rolled to a stop in a space near the emergency entrance.

Ken Callahan gave an audible sigh of relief. The Rottweiler looked around expectantly and thumped his tail against the upholstery.

For some reason Chris suddenly felt annoyed that everyone was so happy to have arrived at their destination. It was as if they were overjoyed at the prospect of quitting her company. Not very complimentary, especially since she was unaccountably depressed at the thought of leaving Ken Callahan. "Hmmph," she snapped."

"Hmmph?"

"You and your dog are obviously ecstatic to see my driving come to an end."

"You drive like a maniac. And besides, you've been fondling me for fifteen minutes. How much do you think a man can take?"

"Fondling you?" she squeaked. "Of all the . . . I never . . . you . . . "

"Oh, man, now I've got you all upset. Listen, I know this is a small truck, and you probably didn't mean to fondle me, but . . . "

"I don't drive like a maniac. I've never driven a truck before." She shook her finger at him. "You haven't made it any easier—you and your dumb dog—and let me assure you that if I fondled you it was purely accidental."

"Yeah, and it was accidental that you broke my arm," he teased.

"You didn't move fast enough!"

He grinned sheepishly. "You're right. I'm not at my best this morning. I didn't get much sleep last night." He leaned toward her and nuzzled her hair. "It wasn't entirely my fault, you know. I was distracted. You looked downright wanton . . . leaning over the engine at me."

Wanton? Of all the nerve, she huffed to herself. She might have been ogling a little, but she definitely hadn't been wanton—had she? "I wasn't feeling wanton. I was concerned about my car."

"Your voice was husky." His lips brushed against her neck as he spoke. His warm breath whispered along tingling skin.

Chris felt her stomach lurch. "My voice is always husky in the morning," she lied. "I wasn't awake, yet. I didn't have time for coffee."

He kissed the nape of her neck, sending a shiver rocketing along her spine. He leaned against her and placed a nibbling sort of kiss just below her earlobe while rain drummed on the roof of the truck, wrapping them in cozy isolation. Chris wondered why she was sitting there, waiting to be kissed again. She had dated sporadically since her divorce, mostly to appease well-meaning friends, and she'd always found herself counting the minutes before she could issue the perfunctory good-night kiss and get home to her daughter. *Why on earth am I feeling so attracted to this man? I don't even know him. I literally picked him up at the side of the road.* She felt a little hysterical.

Ken slipped his hand inside the red vest, his fingers

curled around Chris's rib cage, his thumb resting against the swell of her small breast. "Chris Nelson," he whispered silkily, "you're a very dangerous lady." His thick black lashes lowered as his gaze dropped to her lips.

Chris felt her body turn toward him, desire creeping through her like heated honey. His lips grazed hers in a kiss that was featherlight and lingering.

"Mmmmm . . ." she purred—and then wondered who'd just made that incredibly contented sound. Surely, it wasn't Chris Nelson. Chris Nelson was a dedicated professional, an intrepid mother. Up to now, the only thing capable of evoking that sort of response in Chris Nelson was her mother's New York cheesecake. She sat up with a jolt, surprising both man and dog. The Rottweiler stopped panting momentarily and eyed her suspiciously.

Ken Callahan drew his eyebrows together in a small frown. "Now what?" he asked warily.

"You're trying to seduce me in a hospital parking lot."

"What's wrong with that?"

What's wrong with it is that it's working, she thought. "I don't even know you. And it's inappropriate. And . . ." She was babbling. Grasping at straws. "And your dog is watching."

A look of disbelief registered on Ken Callahan's face. It changed to a smile. He tipped his head back and laughed triumphantly. "I'm really getting to you, huh?"

She pressed her lips together in annoyance. "Doesn't your arm hurt anymore?"

"Not nearly as much as my heart," he confessed playfully.

She opened the truck door and jumped out into the rain, ran the short distance to the emergency entrance, and stood just inside the lobby, shaking out her wet hair and stomping the water off her sneakered feet. She pointed toward the desk. "Why don't you go and register. I have to find a phone. I'm late for work."

"It's five-thirty in the morning. What sort of job do you have? Delivering newspapers? Making doughnuts? Hit man for the mob on the early-morning shift?"

"I'm a skate coach. The rink opens at five-twenty so the kids can practice before school starts."

He studied her slim, compact body and nodded. "It's easy to imagine you on the ice. I'm afraid I'm not very knowledgeable about ice skating—are you famous?"

Chris paused to look at him. His eyes were guileless and filled with genuine curiosity. "I suppose I was several years ago, but I'm not any longer. I might have a certain amount of recognition among other skaters, but my name is hardly a household word these days." She realized she'd left her purse in the athletic bag in the truck and started a fruitless search through the pockets of her vest.

Ken placed a quarter in the palm of her hand. "I assume this is what you're looking for." He grabbed her elbow as she turned away. "Get back to me as fast as you can," he pleaded, "I hate hospitals."

When Chris returned, she found Ken Callahan slouched in a chair, his long legs stretched in front of him. His arm had been put in a sling, and he looked up at her anxiously over a cup of coffee. "You've been gone for hours—what took you so long?"

"I've been gone for five minutes."

He smiled boyishly, slightly embarrassed. "Well, it seemed like hours. They've already taken X rays." He pointed to a Styrofoam cup on the table beside him. "I got you some coffee."

Chris removed the lid and added a container of cream, then studied him as she sipped at the coffee. He had high cheekbones, a perfectly straight nose, and a few flecks of gray in the unruly profusion of wavy black hair. He had a wide mouth, which she could easily imagine set in ruthless determination, but right now he stared moodily into his coffee, the corners of his mouth turned down, and Chris wondered why he was looking so grim. "Is something wrong?"

"To tell you the truth . . . I'm scared to death. I've never been in a hospital before. And I've never broken anything that was mine. Will it hurt?"

Chris gaped in astonishment. He was serious. He really

was scared. She smiled and shook her head. "I don't think it will hurt."

"Have you ever broken anything?"

"When I was a little girl we lived on a farm in Colorado—not a working farm, we just called it a farm because it was eleven acres, and it had a barn. When my parents bought the farm it came complete with a big old black horse named Looney. He was a great horse, but every now and then he liked to see me go over a fence solo. He'd run right up to a fence, plant his feet, and I'd go soaring off into the air. One time I crashed into a split rail and broke my nose."

Ken slowly ran the tip of his finger along the bridge of her nose. "It's a pretty little nose. Straight until the very end, where it tips up just a bit. Elegant without being boring."

She felt her heart flop at his touch, and an unaccountable tingle ran down her spine. "Mmmm," she answered, waiting for her mind to clear. "And then when I was eight I was dancing in my room with a laundry basket on my head . . . and I tripped over a roller skate and broke my arm."

"I find that surprisingly easy to believe."

"And when I was twelve, I broke my finger playing softball."

"Never been hurt skating?"

"Bruises. Lots of bruises. Nothing serious."

"Did you ever compete?"

"For years and years. I was National Novice champion at sixteen, Junior champion when I was eighteen, and National Senior bronze and silver medalist. And then I quit."

He watched her quietly. Their mutual silence grew uncomfortable, the inevitable question hanging ominously suspended in the air between them.

Chris sighed. "Don't you want to know why I quit? Everyone always does."

"I thought it might be sensitive."

She smiled at him, pleasantly surprised at his perception. "It was a long time ago. As a young athlete I'd led a very narrow life. Up at five in the morning. In bed by nine at night. I was the world's latest bloomer. I'd never had any sort of relationship with a boy until I was twenty-one. And that relationship resulted in my daughter, Lucy."

He drained his cup of coffee and returned it to the table. His hand found hers and traced a line along her ring finger. "Want to tell me about the father?"

"Steven Black."

He whistled softly. "The actor?"

"The classic whirlwind courtship. He wined and dined me for two weeks. I thought I was madly in love." She shrugged with her hand. "We were married in a thirty-second service in Las Vegas. Four weeks later I discovered I was pregnant, and my adoring husband divorced me while I was still in my first trimester."

He raised his eyebrows in astonishment. "Why did he do that?"

"Steven wanted a glamorous wife. If I'd stayed with skating I would have been on the Olympic team. Eight years ago Steven was still struggling for recognition, and I suppose he thought he could use the media coverage. When I refused to have an abortion and told him I was giving up competing, he divorced me."

Ken slid his hand along hers and gripped her wrist. Little prickles of pleasure ran up her arm at his possessive touch. His hand was large—a working man's hand, she decided. Strong. Permanently tan. It was a hand that could be gentle and protective and still manipulate with confident authority. In a sudden flash of insight Chris knew what it would be like to share a bed with Ken Callahan. A burst of unexpected heat rushed through her at the thought, and a scarlet scald crept from her shirt collar.

Ken regarded her with serious curiosity. "It must have been difficult for you to give up competing."

Chris smiled. "It was easy. I loved to skate, but I hated to compete. I threw up before every competition. And as soon as I became pregnant my whole body oozed content-ment." She sat forward in her seat, warming to her subject. "Having a baby is a miracle." Her face glowed with satis-faction and pride. "They have fat little hands and tiny fin-gernails, and they love you . . . just because you're there, and you're Mommy. Babies don't care if you're famous or rich."

She felt his hand tighten on hers and knew she had allowed some of the hurt of rejection to surface. She hadn't meant to show that to him. She hadn't even known herself that it still existed. She hurried to cover the slip. "My favorite part of the day is when Lucy and I read bedtime stories. The book I like best is about this little bear. He gets a bicycle, and his father is going to teach him how to ride it, but the father does everything wrong! And then there's another Little Bear book where Little Bear and his dad go hiking with the bear scouts—" Chris stopped suddenly and closed her eyes with a groan. "I don't believe I'm telling you about Little Bear."

His voice was mockingly serious, but his dark eyes danced with amusement. "Little Bear is undoubtedly an important part of your life."

"Are you laughing at me again?"

He put his hand to her cheek. "No. I think it's very nice."

A white-coated intern appeared before them. "Mr. Callahan? I have the results of your X rays. You have a simple fracture. It's not terribly serious, but it'll require a cast. You can go to an orthopedist of your choice, or I can have a staff doctor paged for you. I believe Dr. Wiley is on the floor somewhere."

"Dr. Wiley will be fine."

A bank of steel-gray clouds hung low in the early-morning sky, diffusing the sunlight and adding a chill to the air. Ken Callahan brandished his pristine white, spanking-new cast, like a flag—holding it high to prevent his arm from swelling.

"Keep it above your heart for a few days," Dr. Wiley had advised.

"Above my heart," Ken mumbled, heading for his truck in long, angry strides. "Damned inconvenience." He stopped and looked down at his plaster-clad arm. The cast stretched from his elbow to the middle of his hand, wrapping around his thumb, and making it impossible to grasp anything with his left hand. He wiggled his fingers pathetically. "Just look at this," he ranted. "How can I drive? How can I work? How can I tie my damned shoes?"

Chris trotted beside him. She inserted the key into the locked truck door and bit her lip to keep from laughing. Ken Callahan had ceased to frighten her. He wasn't as disreputable as she'd originally assumed. He was well-spoken and easy to talk to. A little over-sexed, perhaps, but not weird or dangerous. And she knew from the past two hours that his anger was short-lived. He was not a man that held a grudge or nursed a wound—and the memory of him locking her hand in a death grip while his cast was being applied sent spasms of laughter choking in her throat. Her hilarity ceased when she opened the door and came face-to-snout with the Rottweiler. There was a tug at Chris's vest collar and warm breath skimmed along her neck.

"I can hardly wait for first gear," Ken murmured into her ear.

"You weren't so crazy about first gear when we pulled in here."

"I was worried about being driven to the police station."

"And you're not worried anymore?"

"I've decided to take my chances."

Chris wrinkled her nose at him. "Well you needn't be concerned. It's light out. I can see what I'm doing, now. Your honor is perfectly safe." He was a nice man, but she was going to be extra careful about first gear. She didn't have the time or desire to complicate her life with a man. She slid behind the wheel and turned to him. "I suppose I should drive you somewhere. Home? Or to work? Where were you going this morning?"

"I was starting a new job. I wanted to get in early and take a look around before anyone else showed up."

"Oh, no," she groaned, "first day on the job, and I broke your arm." She looked at the jeans and scuffed boots. He had removed his sweat shirt in deference to the cast, leaving him in a yellow short-sleeved T-shirt, which said CONSTRUCTION WORKERS USE THEIR TOOLS. The shirt clung to a flat stomach and broad, muscled chest, the sleeves spanning well-defined biceps. His forearm was

corded, the back covered with a silk mat of black hair.
There was no doubt in Chris's mind that he could crack a
walnut as easily as an egg. Her eyes glazed over in silent
admiration.

"Earth to Chris."

"Uh, I was just wondering about your shirt. You do
construction work?"

"Yeah."

Not a laborer, she decided. He didn't seem the sort to
take orders. A project manager or a supervisor, maybe.
Certainly someone who worked in the field. He didn't get
all those muscles sitting behind a desk. "Should I take you
to work?"

He looked at the cast. "I think I'll pass on work today."

"Won't someone be upset if you don't show up?"

"Relieved would probably be a better word."

The truck idled at a standstill in the parking lot. "That's
a strange thing to say. Are you insecure?" she joked.

He shook his head. "No. I'm ruthless."

An inadvertent shiver ran down her spine at the bitter
tone in his voice.

"And I'm disreputable," he teased, trying to lighten the
conversation.

"It's the stubble."

He rubbed his hand across his whiskered chin.
"Twenty-eight of my last forty-eight hours have been spent
on a plane. And only three of the remaining twenty hours
were spent sleeping. I was afraid to take a razor to my face
at four-thirty this morning."

"Where did you fly in from?"

"Everywhere." She felt him slump in the seat next to
her. He passed a hand through his hair and sighed. "I've
been to three countries and seven cities in the last forty-
eight hours. Six job sites. This would have been number
seven. Maybe I'm glad you broke my arm. I think I'm
running on empty."

"Are you some sort of troubleshooter?"

"Troubleshooter? I guess that's as good a name as any,
but lately I feel more like a trouble*maker*." He quirked a

smile at her. "I'd like to make a pass at you, but all of a sudden, I'm so tired I can hardly keep my eyes open."

"Would you like me to drive you home?"

"I don't think I have a home." It was a flat statement issued in a voice totally devoid of emotion. "There's this place out in Loudoun County where I stay sometimes."

"Loudoun County! After I drop you off, how will I ever get back here? Loudoun County is miles away. There aren't any buses running to Loudoun County, there isn't a subway running to Loudoun County, what are you doing living in Loudoun County?"

He sat with his black curls resting against the rear window, his eyes closed in exhaustion, his cast propped in a ridiculous position on the head of the Rottweiler. "You could spend the night," he smiled dreamily. "It's lonely in Loudoun County."

"I'll pass on the night stuff, but I guess I çan drive you home. After all, you did try to help me."

"Mmmmm."

Chris glanced at her watch. "I have students waiting for me right now. Would you mind hanging around at the skating rink for a couple hours? I'll be done at ten-thirty, and then I can make arrangements with one of the other coaches to follow us out and bring me back home."

"Mmmmm."

Chris looked at him suspiciously. "Did you hear anything I said?" There was no response. He was asleep.

Chapter Two

CHRIS DRIED HER skate blades and put the custom Harlicks in her locker. She slipped her feet into her tennis shoes and wondered about the man and dog she'd left slumbering in the parking lot. She'd treated them equally, cracking a window for ventilation and covering them with a blanket from the coaches' lounge. Toward the end of her last lesson she'd had visions of man and beast perishing—like the little match girl—frozen to death under a mantle of dog-induced frost. She pushed through the heavy lobby door and stared horrified into the parking lot. There was no truck. There was no trace of Ken Callahan. No dog.

Bitsy Schoffit barged through the doors behind her. "Okay, I'm ready to go."

Chris spread her arms in a gesture of confusion. "He isn't here. The truck is gone."

"I thought he couldn't drive."

"I dunno. Maybe he called someone to come and get him while I was on the ice." She clapped her hand to her forehead. "And he's got my purse. I left it in the truck."

Bitsy shook her head and made motherly clucking sounds with her tongue. "Dumb, dumb, dumb."

"It's not so bad. He probably got someone to take him home and didn't realize the purse was on the floor. I'll just go home and call the hospital. They can give me his phone number."

Bitsy unlocked the door to her BMW, motioned for Chris to get in, and plunked her own small body into the plush red seat. At forty-three she was still slim and graceful on ice, moving effortlessly with her students through difficult choreography. On land she was an ox. On land she stomped and plunked and stumbled with unconscious abandon.

Bitsy turned the BMW onto Little River Turnpike. Half a mile up the road the two women simultaneously spotted Chris's abandoned tan hatchback on the far shoulder. They gave it a cursory glance, as if it belonged to some unknown person, and continued on to the next light.

"Old news," Chris said finally—her thoughts returning to the car.

Bitsy was familiar with the Chris Nelson philosophy of car care. "Time to buy a new one, huh?"

"Five weeks too early. I have my money tied up in a T-bill that doesn't mature for five more weeks."

Bitsy gave another series of clucks. "Tsk, tsk, tsk." She pulled into Chris's subdivision and rolled to a stop in front of her house. "Let me guess," she said, pointing to the blue pickup parked at the curb. "Is this the phantom truck?"

"Oh no! What's he doing here?"

Bitsy giggled. "I imagine he's in there having tea with Aunt Edna."

"Just what I need. Edna's convinced I should remarry. Remember poor John Farrell? And last week she arranged a date for me with the guy who came to read our electric meter. Edna'll take one look at Ken Callahan and think she's gone to matchmakers' heaven."

"Wow. That nice?"

"An eleven, no sweat. And I don't want to have anything to do with him. I like my life just the way it is." Chris slammed the car door behind her and took twelve feet of sidewalk in two strides. She turned, waved at Bitsy, and hammered on her front door.

Aunt Edna bellowed, "Hold your pants on," and glared out above a security chain. "Well, good golly," she complained, "what with all that thundering, I thought it had to be some lunatic escaped from Lorton prison. Why didn't you just use your key?"

"It's in my purse, and I don't have my purse with me." Chris pushed past Edna. "Where is he?"

"You mean that nice Ken Callahan?"

Chris moved from the foyer to the living room, to the dining room. She felt her patience evaporating and clenched her teeth to keep from shouting. "Yes. 'That nice Ken Callahan.' Where is he?"

Aunt Edna blocked the doorway between living room and dining room. She stood five feet tall in sensible sturdy brown shoes, and her snow-white hair was tightly curled in rows marching obediently across her gleaming pink skull. She had snapping blue eyes—and a body like a fireplug. "It was just like Goldilocks," she cried, slapping her leg. "I took Lucy to school, and when I came home there he was —sleeping in your bed."

Chris felt her voice rise to a shriek. "In my bed?"

"He's such a nice man, dear. And he looked so peaceful, tucked under your big down quilt."

She opened her eyes wide in a mixture of outrage and disbelief. "Under my quilt?"

The stairs creaked behind Chris, and she whirled around as Ken sauntered into the room, looking sleepily sexy and perfectly at home.

"I don't know how two tiny women can make so much noise," he mumbled. "What's all the racket about?"

"*You!* How did you get in here? And what were you doing in my bed?"

He rubbed the back of his neck and grinned. Evidently remembering his cast, he diligently raised it above his heart. "Dog and I just about froze to death in the truck. I was going to come inside the skating rink to get warm, but I was afraid I looked too disreputable, so I fished around in your purse until I found your address and your keys, and then I drove myself over here."

"I thought you couldn't drive."

"Well, I discovered I could just about wrap my fingers around the wheel." He waved his cast at her and wiggled his fingers. "And lucky it was my left arm that you broke, because I can shift with my good hand."

"And then you just let yourself in and went to bed?" she sputtered.

"There wasn't anyone home."

"It was just like Goldilocks," Aunt Edna insisted. "I went upstairs and there he was, sleeping just as peaceful as could be."

"Until Edna started screaming." He raised an eyebrow at Edna. "You've got some voice."

Edna sniffed indignantly. "Well, what do you think? You think I'm some frail old lady? And if you hadn't come up with a good explanation I'd have cracked your skull wide open with my wooden rolling pin."

Chris smiled and looked sidewise at Ken Callahan. "Don't doubt it for a minute," she whispered.

"You're obviously closely related."

"Aunt Edna is my mother's sister and reigning family matriarch."

"Seventy-five years old, and I'm almost as good as new," she said proudly. "Now you young folks go into the parlor, and I'll get us some refreshments."

"That won't be necessary, Aunt Edna. I'm sure Mr. Callahan will be anxious to be on his way."

Aunt Edna's mouth closed with a determined snap. "I won't hear of it. Anyone can see the man is hungry, and he don't look like he's in such a hurry to leave."

Ken beamed. "I'd like to stay for refreshments."

"You see?" Edna gloated. "I knew he didn't want to rush off." She smacked her lips with satisfaction and bustled off to the kitchen.

Ken chuckled softly. "I like your aunt."

Chris glanced up at him. "When my marriage collapsed it was Aunt Edna that put the pieces back together. Her own husband died eleven years ago. When I was in my eighth month, Aunt Edna arrived unannounced and informed me that I needed looking after. I was the only one in my Lamaze class with a sixty-seven-year-old lady for a coach." Chris shook her head, still amazed at the memory.

"She went right through delivery with me. She was wonderful."

"And she's lived with you ever since?"

"Off and on. She travels from family member to family member. Mostly wherever there's a disaster. Lately I've tried to keep her here because of Lucy. In order for me to make enough money to support us it's necessary for me to give after-school and evening lessons. If it weren't for Aunt Edna, I'd have to put Lucy in day care and hire babysitters at night."

Ken relaxed onto the couch and patted the spot next to him. "Come sit by me." The sounds of banging cupboards and clanking dishes drifted in from the kitchen. Ken looked in the direction of the clatter. His mouth twitched and finally gave way to a full-fledged grin.

"What's so funny?"

"I just thought of something your aunt said to me." He threw his head back and laughed.

Chris marveled at the quality of his laughter. It was full and rich and deeply masculine and impossible to ignore. She smiled and prodded him. "Well? What did she say?"

"When she walked in and found me asleep in your bed, she let out with this ear-splitting screech—it had me sitting bolt upright before I even opened my eyes. But then she took a good look at me. I guess she sized me up and figured I was okay, because her first words were . . . 'Merciful heavens, there's finally a man in my niece's bed.'"

"I'll kill her."

"I get the impression that your aunt would like to see you married."

"That's the understatement of the century. She's fixed me up with meter readers, shoe salesmen, a fat fifty-two-year-old butcher, and last week she scared the bejeebers out of John Farrell."

"Who's John Farrell?"

"My accountant." Chris waved her hand in a dismissing gesture. "As soon as Aunt Edna found out John was single she did everything but produce my dental records and promise a dowry. I love Aunt Edna, but she's entirely guileless, and she gets more outspoken as she gets older.

She says she hasn't got much time left, so she's not going to spend it pussyfooting around."

"Edna ever find John Farrell in your bed?"

"No!" Chris rolled her eyes at the thought. She couldn't imagine pleasant, innocuous John Farrell in her bed. She took a stealthy breath and reluctantly admitted to herself that she could easily imagine Ken Callahan there.

Edna trotted in with a plate of cookies. "Are you talking about that John Farrell?" She narrowed her eyes at Ken. "What a wimp. Had him over to dinner and he picked at his roast beef. Didn't eat his peas at all." She shook her head in dismay. "That man had no spirit. No backbone." She winked at Ken and smiled broadly at Chris. "Now this one here is more like it. This guy's got something to him."

Chris sighed and selected a cookie. Once Aunt Edna got started there was no stopping her. Might as well sit back and watch him squirm, she thought, taking a perverse delight in the possibility that Ken and Edna deserved each other. After all, it wasn't as if she had any future plans for Ken Callahan. She wouldn't ever see him again—might as well let Aunt Edna have some fun with him.

"Are you married?" Edna asked.

"Nope."

Edna looked appalled. "A big, strapping man like you —not married? And you're not getting any younger. How old are you?"

"Thirty-six."

Edna took an Oreo. She broke it in half and nibbled the white icing off one of the wafers. "You're not one of those men that prefers boys, are you?"

Ken Callahan choked on his Ovaltine. "No ma'am! I'm . . . uh . . . old-fashioned about that kind of stuff."

Chris covered her mouth to keep from giggling. This promised to be even better than the demolition of John Farrell.

Edna leaned forward in eager anticipation. "You got a steady job?"

Ken turned to Chris; his eyes danced with diabolical delight. The silent message was blatant: Feed me to the wolves, will you? When he turned back to Edna his face was a solemn mask. "I was supposed to start a new job today, but as you can see..." He waved his arm pathetically in front of him. "I've got a broken arm. I can't work with this cast on."

Edna sucked in her breath. "And all because you stopped to help my niece. Isn't that noble? Don't that beat all?"

Chris pressed herself deeper into the sofa cushions and surreptitiously made a motion that said she might gag. "Noble," she croaked.

Ken Callahan stole a smug look in Chris's direction. He toyed with a vanilla wafer.

"What a pity," Edna went on. "How will you get by?"

"I have some savings."

"A man with a savings account. Now that's character," she told her niece. "Seems a shame to have to dip into your savings on account of us. I feel just terrible about this."

A knot was developing in Chris's stomach. This wasn't taking the usual course. By this time Aunt Edna should have had him in a sweat, but Ken Callahan was looking more pleased by the minute. And he was planning something sneaky—Chris was sure of it.

Ken stretched and relaxed deeper into the couch. "This is a nice room."

Chris blinked at the sudden change in conversation. There was none of the earlier affectation. He seemed genuinely impressed. *I don't trust him,* she thought. He'd been leading up to something. She sat up warily and paid close attention, watching his eyes as they observed the room.

It was an airy room with eggshell walls and matching sheers. The plush wall-to-wall carpeting was a warm beige tone. The few pieces of furniture were comfortably overstuffed and covered in earth-tone tans with the exception of a cocoa-and-white houndstooth check wingback chair. The subdued colors provided the perfect background for gregarious Boston ferns, delicate asparagus ferns, potted fig trees, basketed orange trees, hanging ivies, and a colorful collection of African violets in traditional clay pots. The plants seemed to begin in the living room, randomly sprinkled here and there, picking up momentum and becoming more dense as they progressed toward the dining room, where they converged around the patio doors.

Ken's attention focused on a cluster of photographs. "Do you mind if I look at the pictures in your dining room?"

Aunt Edna jumped to her feet. "You want to see the pictures?"

Chris groaned. This was not a good sign.

"This here's a photograph of some sailing ships. Chris got this when we went vacationing in Maine last year. And this here's a picture of me when I was a little girl. Wasn't I a pip? Just look at those ribbed stockings. This is an elephant at the zoo, and this is a picture Lucy drew when we come home."

Ken looked at the crayon drawing of a smiling elephant. It had been framed and matted with the same professional care as all the other pictures. He tilted his head in Chris's direction. "Your daughter must feel very special to have her drawing on this wall."

Chris caught her breath at the enigmatic softening in his eyes, the tender huskiness of his voice.

Edna puffed up with pride. "It's a beauty of an elephant, isn't it? She can draw anything. She's got real talent."

"Like her mom." Ken smiled at Edna.

"The spitting image." Edna pointed to a photograph of a little girl hanging upside down from a tree limb. Her orange hair hung in wild curls that hadn't seen a comb all day. She wore pink shorts, smudged with mud. Her sneakers were battered, her shoelaces untied, and she was laughing and closing her eyes tight in childish abandon.

Ken laughed with the photograph. "Is this Lucy?"

"Yep. But it might as well have been her mother. She looked just like that when she was seven."

His attention wandered to the bowl of cut flowers in the middle of the dining room table. He ran his finger over the table's freshly polished surface. "You've done a lot to make this a home. I wish I had a home like this."

Little alarm bells sounded in Chris's brain. There was a

genuine wistfulness to his voice, which she didn't doubt, but his eyes were filled with mischief and cunning.

"Haven't you got a home?" Edna exclaimed.

He shook his head. "I've been doing a lot of traveling because of my job. I haven't had much time to gather the things together that make a house a home."

"Maybe Chris could help you. Where do you live? Do you have a house of your own?"

"There's this place out in Loudoun County where I stay sometimes."

"Loudoun County. That's a ride."

He nodded. "It would be much more convenient for me if I lived around here." He delicately draped his good arm around Edna's shoulders. "I have a confession to make. Ever since I walked into this house, I've been toying with an idea. I have two problems—I haven't got a homey place to live, and I can't go to work for a while. You and Chris also have two problems—you haven't got a car, and you haven't got an abundance of money. I noticed that you have an extra bedroom and bath downstairs—maybe we could work out some kind of deal. The use of my truck, plus"—he waved his hand while he contemplated a sum—"fifty dollars a week. We could be roomies."

Chris sprang from the couch. *"No!"*

Edna stood firm with her hands on her hips. "I think it's a wonderful idea."

"We don't even know this man."

"I know all I need to know. This house needs a man underfoot." Edna smacked her lips and narrowed her eyes in determination. "Do you take out garbage?" she asked Ken.

"Yes, ma'am."

"You see?" she informed her niece. "He'll be perfect."

"He'll be a perfect pain in the . . ."

Edna raised her eyebrows in warning. She didn't allow any cussing.

". . . in the foot. And what about Lucy?"

Now Ken Callahan raised his eyebrows. "What about Lucy?"

"It wouldn't look right."

"Pshaw," Edna scoffed. "Women have been taking in boarders for centuries."

Chris glared at the man standing smugly in front of her. "I would like to speak with you privately, in the kitchen," she hissed.

"Will you excuse us?" he said pleasantly to Aunt Edna.

Chris growled and stomped off to the kitchen. She closed the louvered kitchen door with a slam and turned to face Ken Callahan. "Let's get something perfectly straight, Ken Callahan. I have no intention of allowing you to live in this house. I think it's despicable of you to wheedle your way around my Aunt Edna, and I wouldn't trust you for a second with my daughter."

An expression of amused disgust played on his face. "That's a bunch of baloney. Your Aunt Edna is a nice old barracuda who only gets wheedled when she wants to. And it's not your daughter you're worried about—it's you."

Chris pressed her lips together in annoyance. He was right. She'd had a nice sane life—until this morning—and she didn't want it disrupted. And Ken Callahan could definitely disrupt. He was much too handsome. Much too sexy. And every now and then there was a flash of genuine vulnerability that broke down all her defenses. She had avoided romantic entanglements for the last seven years without feeling any real sense of loss. It was safe. It was comfortable. It was a way of life that would crumble with Ken Callahan lurking in her kitchen—wearing those form-fitting faded jeans. She decided to take the coward's way out and ignore his accusations. She rallied to a new attack. "Why are you doing this?"

"I need a place to live."

"There are dozens of ads in the paper every day looking for roommates."

"That's true, but I like it here." He surveyed the kitchen, his gaze drifting from the blond butcher-block countertops with the brown teddy bear cookie jar and the assortment of clear glass jars filled with spaghetti, sugar, whole oats, macaroni, popcorn, and flour to a Peter Rabbit place setting stacked in the sink. A bulletin board and chalkboard had been hung on one wall—the chalkboard was at the proper height for a seven-year-old. Ken picked up a piece of colored chalk and drew a straight line across the green surface. He studied the line for a moment, seemingly intrigued by the textured mark. Almost reluctantly, he returned the chalk to its wooden carrier and turned to Chris, putting his hand on her shoulder in a possessive caress that lingered briefly then moved to her neck. His finger touched an earlobe and slid along the curve of her jaw. "And I like you. I don't know why. You're kind of crusty. And you're too skinny. But there's something about you that makes my toes curl."

"What do you mean crusty and skinny? I'm not at all crusty, and I'm certainly not skinny."

He stepped closer, smiling broadly, obviously pleased that he'd provoked her. Chris felt the warmth from his body swirl around her, and the kitchen temperature seemed to rise twenty degrees. He continued to trail a path along her chin. When his finger reached her mouth, she instinctively licked her dry lips, inadvertently touching the tip of her tongue to the tip of his finger. Their reactions were totally different but equally swift. Chris jumped away as if she'd been burned. How could less than five seconds of contact do that to her stomach? she agonized. It was like falling forty floors in an elevator.

Ken Callahan's stomach seemed to be made of sterner stuff. He smiled wolfishly and pressed himself against her, pinning her to the wall. "I realize that lovely little lick was just a reflex action, but I'm going to take advantage of it anyway," he whispered cheerfully.

"Don't you dare!"

"I can't help myself. Kitchens always have this romantic effect on me."

"Keep away from me, or I'll bop you on the head with Aunt Edna's rolling pin."

"Wouldn't you like to be kissed in the kitchen?" he teased.

"No."

"Are you sure? I'm a terrific kisser."

The man is evil, Chris decided. *He knows he can raise my blood pressure just by dropping his voice an octave, and he's absolutely enjoying it.* She pushed against his chest with both hands, hoping he wouldn't feel her heart pounding in her chest. "You're horrid."

"I like when your voice gets all husky and tremulous like that." His cobalt eyes lowered as he played with the zipper on her sweat suit jacket. "There's a nice chemistry between us. You knew it as soon as I did—when we looked at each other under the hood of your car. For some reason it scares the heck out of you."

"I don't want to get involved."

"I know that. That's why I'm moving in."

"What?"

"If I did the normal thing and asked you out to dinner, would you go out with me?"

"No."

"I didn't think so. So I'll live here." He smoothed the rumples from the front of her warm-up suit. "Besides, it will be convenient for both of us. I really do need a place to stay. I'm tired of shifting around. I need a home—even if it's someone else's home. And you need the money and the transportation. A match made in heaven."

Oh boy, she thought, *I'm doomed. Putty in his hands.* "Do you know what a glamus is?"

"A what?"

"Never mind. I suppose you can stay." She sighed. "Aunt Edna has her mind made up, anyway." Suddenly she felt very, very tired. "But I'm serious about not getting involved. Keep your distance."

"Or you'll drive me straight to the police station."

Chris felt her lips twitch in spite of herself. "You're laughing at me, again."

"Maybe a little." His hand touched her waist and boldly slid under the top to her warm-up suit. He flattened his palm against her bare stomach, the tips of his fingers touching the bottommost part of her breast. His eyes grew dark and liquid. "But it's a nice kind of laughing."

She knew it was a nice kind of laughing. It was gentle and good-humored and affectionate . . . very affectionate. He was everything she didn't want to find in a man. He was lovable. And the feel of his hand on her stomach was exquisite. She was sure that when he removed the hand she would be branded for life—that she would never forget the delicious sensations emanating through her body as his fingers splayed across her heated flesh.

There was a flurry of obtrusive plate clanking and throat clearing in the living room. "What's going on in there?" Edna called. "It's awfully quiet."

Ken deposited a quick, light kiss on Chris's lips and the muted hunger in his eyes shifted to amusement. "I don't think you have to worry about this arrangement. I think Aunt Edna could be a formidable chaperone."

Aunt Edna bustled through the kitchen door, the plates and glasses clattering noisily in her hands. "I hate being left out of stuff. If you're going to talk in the kitchen, then you're going to have to talk louder."

Chris took the dishes and began stacking them in the dishwasher. "We were just coming to terms with this— boarding arrangement."

Ken managed to steal a cookie before they were whisked away into the teddy bear cookie jar. "The deal is that I take out the garbage, and I mind my manners."

Aunt Edna nodded in approval. "Dinner is at six. You can have the run of the refrigerator between meals—as long as you don't eat us out of house and home. Goodness, it's nice to have a man in the house." She grinned.

Chris took a key from a hook on the bulletin board. She studied the key for a moment, contemplating the significance of the act. She suspected she was giving Ken Callahan more than just the key to her house. She was giving him the chance to wreak havoc with her life—and she didn't doubt for a second that he would take advantage of the opportunity. So, why am I doing this? she agonized. Because I need his truck, she answered. Because I need his money. Chris considered the key innocently resting in the palm of her hand. Were there other reasons? Because he was incredibly handsome? Because he could be outrageously endearing? *Because when he's close to me it's like lying in the sun—all sizzling skin and luscious heat that sinks straight to my soul.* Chris made an effort to control the shiver that ran along her spine, and presented him with the key. "This is for the front door."

Ken extracted a key ring from his jeans pocket and attempted to work a key loose. The key ring fell from his hand and clattered onto the kitchen floor. There was a brief look of dismay at his one-handed helplessness. He sighed and retrieved the keys. "And this is for the truck," he told her, handing her the entire key chain. He lowered his voice to a coaxing whisper. "I'm sorry, Chris, I can't do this by myself. You're going to have to help me."

She felt her pulse falter as she fumbled with the keys. Her eyes avoided his while she wrestled with the double entendre.

"Ain't that nice," Aunt Edna said. "A real ceremony. Just like getting married."

Chris felt the blush creep along the back of her neck. Aunt Edna had the unnerving habit of saying out loud what everyone else was thinking. Chris thought back to the white-gowned pomp of her hastily planned wedding ceremony almost eight years ago. It had been lovely and exciting, but it had lacked the intimacy and intriguing solemnity of this simple kitchen key exchange. It was a frightening and annoying admission to make, but in some inexplicable way, she suddenly felt married to Ken Callahan.

Ken Callahan looked at the two women from under lowered lids as he returned his keys to his pocket. His mouth was stretched into a roguish smile that didn't quite extend to his tired eyes. "I don't think I'd make much of a bridegroom today, Aunt Edna. My arm is starting to ache again, and I'm exhausted."

"Land sakes, you look like you haven't slept in days."

"I haven't." He slouched against the doorjamb and hugged his broken arm. "Don't suppose you'd want to tuck me in?" he asked Chris.

Aunt Edna shook her head. "He sounds frisky, but he doesn't look like he has much spunk left in him. Why don't you show him his room while I fix lunch."

Chris led the way downstairs. The lower level rooms were carpeted in the same plush beige. A comfortably plump russet-colored corduroy couch, bordered by two end tables, faced the large brick fireplace that dominated a corner of the rec room. An oversized coffee table, overflowing with children's books, filled the space between the couch and the fireplace. Two doors led off the family room, one leading to a neat utility room, and the second leading to the guest bedroom and adjoining bath. Chris motioned to the double bed covered with a red plaid comforter. "There are fresh sheets on the bed. I'll bring some extra towels down later."

"Will you read me a bedtime story?" His voice was pleasantly husky with fatigue. "The one about Little Bear?"

Chris touched her finger to his bearded cheek. He was dead on his feet, but he could dredge up enough energy for some gentle teasing. Most men would be grouchy and short-tempered by now. There was something about him—a playfulness, a fleeting glimpse of wistful trust that stirred feelings in her that she'd only before felt for baby birds, orphaned kittens, and sleeping children. It was strange that the most virile, competent male she'd ever met could evoke such tender emotions. Her eyebrows drew together in a scowl. And then there were the times when he was infuriating. Arrogant. Aggressive. Sneaky.

Ken shook his head. "I wouldn't want to guess what just went through your mind. I've never seen emotions parade across anyone's face like that before. One minute you were on the verge of a good night kiss and in a matter of seconds you were considering homicide."

"You're pretty sharp when you're tired."

He flopped down on the bed. "Mmmm, and I'm even better when I'm horizontal."

"You're impossible." Her mood seesawed back to poignant affection. "I'm sorry I broke your arm."

He closed his eyes and smiled. "I'm not."

Chris resisted the urge to help him with his boots. She turned quickly and left the room before he could open his eyes and see the glow of pleasure his words had produced.

Chapter Three

CHRIS SAT IN rush-hour traffic, one hand resting on the leather-wrapped steering wheel of Ken Callahan's custom truck, the other hand pressing against her churning stomach. She'd done something incredibly stupid. She'd allowed Ken Callahan into her house—into her heart. She would have been better off if she'd simply allowed him into her bed. That would have been sex. That would have been something she could handle.

She inched the truck forward in the endless traffic and slumped in her seat. Who was she trying to kid? Sex with Ken Callahan would be a disaster. *I'm like a dinosaur. I'm practically an extinct species. I'm a mental virgin, for Pete's sake.* She couldn't even imagine casual sex. And even if she could divorce sex from love, sex with Ken Callahan would probably ruin her for life—how would she ever top it?

Chris turned left off Little River Turnpike and headed for her subdivision. Her street looked normal enough. Her townhouse seemed just as she'd left it, but she knew it was merely a deceptive facade. Nothing would be normal as long as Ken Callahan had the key to her front door. She parked at the curb and tried to squelch the turmoil in her chest. *This will never work,* she told herself as she hopped from the truck. *He has to go.* She stomped up the sidewalk, berating herself. "How could I ever have agreed to this?" she muttered, throwing her arms in the air. "This is absurd." The front door crashed open and Chris stormed into the room.

"Well, here she is," Aunt Edna said to Ken Callahan. "Just like I told you. Muttering and stomping. All in a dither. Just look at her. Ain't she a pip?"

The last sentence was uttered with such unadulterated pride and love that Ken had to smile in appreciation. He adjusted the little girl on his lap to a more comfortable position and carefully laid a picture book on the coffee table.

Lucy smiled happily and held out her arms for her hello kiss. "Mommy, you're just in time to hear Ken finish the story."

Chris tipped her head in Ken's direction and gave him her most withering stare. "Little Bear?"

"Uh, no. I tried that, but I didn't feel entirely comfortable with a bunch of bears. I found one about a steam shovel. It's about this guy and his old steam shovel, and they've got to finish this job by sundown or . . ." Ken Callahan flushed red under his swarthy skin and dark beard. "I suppose you already know the story," he added with an embarrassed grin.

I'm in big trouble, Chris thought. No woman in her right mind could hold out against that grin, and how could she possibly evict a man when he had her daughter enthralled on his lap? She bolstered her flagging hostility with the thought that this was just a temporary setback. She would kick him out after supper. She would do it the sneaky way—when Lucy and Aunt Edna were in bed and couldn't come to his rescue. Chris walked cautiously across the room to receive her daughter's hug.

Ken watched her approach with obvious delight. His afternoon nap had erased the dark circles around his eyes, and the tension lines had faded from his bearded cheeks. The corners of his mouth twitched with suppressed deviltry. There was no need for him to speak—his crackling blue eyes told her he had won this round and was openly gloating over his victory.

Chris bent to kiss her daughter's orange curls and up-turned nose, unavoidably coming inches from Ken's freshly washed hair. She recognized the lemon-and-lilac scent overlaying a hint of natural masculine musk. He had used her shampoo and bath soap. She paused for a moment, astonished at the wifely feelings this knowledge produced. It seemed perfectly natural and surprisingly intimate. A pang of longing for crushed dreams pierced her heart. It was such a simple thing—the intermingling of male and female fragrance. The realization that it would be forever denied to her was almost more than she could bear, evoking emotions long buried and producing a pain that lodged in her throat like a huge silent sob.

She had always imagined that her marriage would be long and happy—like her parents'—a collection of shared intimacies, communal goals, loving memories. She had jumped at the first man who'd come along because she'd wanted all those things so badly. And she'd ended up with nothing.

No, that wasn't true. She had Lucy. And Lucy had been enough until this Ken Callahan had popped into her life. Damn him. Ken Callahan resurrected tender, hungry feelings that couldn't be trusted. He had the potential to be heartache and grief—and trouble with a capital T.

"This is ridiculous," she mumbled gruffly.

Ken chuckled at her exclamation. His laughter rumbled warm against her ear, and he feathered a kiss against her hair as she bowed her head to hug Lucy. "I'm not sure I follow you," he teased. "Care to elaborate?"

"This whole thing is ridiculous," she hissed in a stage whisper. "And I'll tell you more of what I'm talking about after supper."

She stiffened her back and fled to the kitchen to sort out her emotions. What was wrong with her? How could she be feeling so comfortably bound to a man that she'd picked up on the highway twelve hours ago? And if she did feel so comfortably bound to him, why did he make her so *un*comfortable? The answer to that was obvious. Because he was slick and handsome and too good to be true; another Prince Charming. A Steven Black clone. She pulled four plates from the kitchen cabinet and marched into the dining room. She thumped them on the table.

Lucy, still on Ken's lap, giggled. "Isn't Mommy funny when she's mad? She always makes so much noise."

Chris glared at the two of them, and Ken suppressed a smile. "Maybe we'd better finish this book," he suggested tactfully.

Chris made a frustrated gesture as she swished back through the kitchen doors. Twelve hours ago she'd picked up a construction worker on the highway and now he was living in her house and reading books about steam shovels to her daughter—and very shortly they'd all be sitting around feeling used and abandoned. Chris thrashed around in the silverware drawer. Everyone liked him. Aunt Edna liked him. Lucy liked him. She had to admit it—she even liked him. Why couldn't he have been some frog? Someone everyone hated. Someone that would have been easy to get rid of.

Aunt Edna turned from the stove with a disapproving look for the havoc Chris was causing among the silverware. She paused for effect, her wooden spoon held at half-mast. "He fits right in, don't he?"

"Mmmph," Chris gurgled, an expletive strangling in her throat. "I don't want him to fit right in. I want him to leave. I liked my life the way it was . . . without a man in my house."

Aunt Edna plopped her spoon back into the spaghetti sauce. "Nonsense. You've lived without a man long enough. Lucy needs a father, and you need a husband."

"I've already had a husband, and I didn't like it."

"That horse's rump wasn't a husband. Spent the whole day looking in the mirror, fixing his hair."

"What makes you think Ken Callahan's any better?"

The old woman wiped her hands on her apron and faced her niece. "I'm not real book smart, and every now and then I worry I'm getting a little senile, but I've got some common sense, and I know something about people. Ken Callahan is a good man. He's got gentleness and humor." Edna turned back to the stove, then shot her niece a side-wise look and smiled broadly. "And he's got a great body."

"Aunt Edna!"

"I might be old, but I know a great body when I see one. Uh-huh!"

Chris threw her head back and burst out laughing. She crossed the kitchen and hugged her aunt. "You're right, as always—he does have a great body."

Ken pushed through the kitchen door and snatched a breadstick from the glass jar on the counter. "So, you think I have a great body, huh?"

Chris grimaced. "God is really out to get me today."

"Don't be blasphemous," Edna warned.

Ken looked sadly at the cast on his arm. "My body used to be perfect."

I don't doubt it for a second, Chris thought.

"This is the second time I've had spaghetti today," Lucy announced. "We had spaghetti for lunch in school." She looked at the plate in front of her, piled with whole-wheat spaghetti noodles and Aunt Edna's chunky homemade sauce. Lucy sprinkled the freshly grated parmesan cheese on her meal with painstaking care. "The spaghetti we had in school was yucky. The noodles were white . . . like dead worms. And it didn't have any sausage in it or nothing. And the sauce was orange and watery. And I didn't eat it."

Ken nodded sympathetically. "What did you do with it, if you didn't eat it?"

Lucy looked at him suspiciously. "How do you know I did something with it?"

"Lucky guess."

Lucy giggled. "I gave it to Tommy Hostrup. Beth Ann Cristo gave hers to him. And Sally Winthrop. And Audrey Schtek. We gave him all our spaghetti, and we told him we'd give him a dollar if he could eat it."

"Did he eat it?"

"He tried, but he couldn't get it all in. It was awful. There were noodles hanging out of his mouth, and he had sauce all down his neck."

"When I was your age they served spaghetti in my school cafeteria, too," Ken told her. "We used to empty our milk cartons and fill them with the spaghetti. Then we'd take the cartons and put them behind the wheel of the principal's station wagon. When he drove away at the end of the day, he'd run over the cartons and all the spaghetti would squish out."

"Oh, gross!"

Ken leaned across the table and whispered to her conspiratorially. "There was this big bully in my school, Larry Newfarmer. He was really fat, and he used to pick on all the little kids. Everybody hated him. One day when we had spaghetti, I got his spelling workbook and put spaghetti noodles between all the pages without him knowing it."

Lucy's eyes got wide, and she clapped a hand over her mouth to control the giggles. "Then what?"

Ken leaned back in his chair and grinned sheepishly. "Then I sat on it. And the noodles got smashed between the pages. And when Larry Newfarmer went to spelling the next morning, those pages were stuck together forever."

Aunt Edna had bent her head and tried not to laugh. "Sh-sh-shame on you!" she managed when she was finally able to speak.

Chris's mouth curved into an unconscious smile. Her family was thoroughly enjoying Ken Callahan, and he seemed to be enjoying them. Other male guests had always politely tolerated Lucy—Ken Callahan actually liked her. Ken Callahan had a place in his heart for childish activities. *That's a nice trait to find in a man*, she thought, watching him in open admiration. He was lean and hard with broad shoulders and muscles in all the right places— but it was his face that intrigued her the most. There was an inherent strength in it. A magnetic confidence that could only be found in a man who had come to terms with himself and was not unhappy with what he saw. The fledgling beard enhanced the aura of virility that radiated from compelling blue eyes and a wide mobile mouth. An easy man to fall in love with, she mused . . . if you were the sort of woman who wanted to fall in love.

Ken raised a forkful of spaghetti to his lips and caught Chris watching him. His eyes searched her face, reaching into her thoughts. She decided to partially oblige him. "I was thinking about Mike Mulligan. You really enjoyed that, didn't you?"

The tips of his ears reddened. "I . . . uh . . . I've always liked steam shovels."

There was a loud rapping at the front door followed by a mournful howl.

Ken looked puzzled. "That sounds like Dog, but I know I left him in the backyard."

Edna got to the door first. "Well, Mrs. Thatcher," she smiled, opening the door wide.

Mrs. Thatcher stood flat-footed and ready for battle on the porch. She held the cowering Rottweiler by the scruff of his neck. "Someone told me this dog came from the truck parked in front of your house. Is this your dog, Edna?"

"I don't know. What's he done?"

"He's dug up every bush in my yard, that's what he's done."

"Then he ain't my dog," Edna told her.

Ken took Edna by the shoulders and removed her from his path. "That's my dog, Mrs. Thatcher."

The huge black beast looked at his owner mournfully. Telltale sprigs of evergreen and pieces of bark clung from his collar.

"I'll be living here for a while," he told the woman. "Have the landscaping repaired, and I'll pay for it."

"Hmmm," she said, handing the dog over to him.

Ken closed the door and shook his finger at the dog. "You were bad."

Lucy bounded over. "A dog! I didn't know you had a dog."

The Rottweiler thumped his tail against the floor. It stood on all fours and looked Lucy in the eye, waggling its body side to side as it followed the happy tail.

Lucy hugged the dog enthusiastically. "What's its name?"

"Dog."

Edna sniffed disapproval. "Dog? What kind of a name is that?"

Ken shrugged. "He was given to me as a puppy a year

ago, and I was so busy I never had time to think of a name. I just always called him Dog."

"Poor creature," Chris murmured, patting the sleek ebony coat. "Imagine if someone named you Human," she scolded Ken.

The slight curve at the corners of his mouth indicated his amusement at her concern. "Would you like to choose a better name? I don't think it's too late." He looked affectionately at the dog. "What do you think? Would you like a new name?"

Lucy looked at Ken with large round eyes. "Could we call him Bob? I always wanted a dog named Bob."

"I think Bob would be a great name for him. Why don't you take Bob into the kitchen and give him a breadstick while I talk to your mom a minute."

They both watched Lucy trot off with the dog. Chris felt Ken step closer to her. An electric flash ran along her spine and tingled at her fingertips. She felt his breath in her hair. "Uh"—she blinked in warm distress—"you wanted to talk to me?"

"Mmmm," he hummed in a raspy whisper, "but the words I want to say to you can't be said in front of Aunt Edna."

Without turning to look, Chris knew Aunt Edna had taken her position in the rocker and was keeping her eye on them. "Thank God for Aunt Edna." Chris laughed shakily.

He leaned away from her and assumed a more casual attitude. "If you don't have plans for the truck tonight, I'd like to make a trip out to Loudoun County. I'll leave Bob there. I think his style might be cramped in a townhouse. And I have to pick up some clothes."

"That would be fine. I don't have any lessons scheduled for tonight."

He whistled and called, "Bob!"

The dog bounded up to him. "He's so smart," he bragged. "You see how he knows his new name already?" He grabbed his vest from the hall coat rack, kissed Chris full on the lips, and swept out the door. Halfway down the sidewalk he turned. "I called your auto club and had them tow the car to a garage. The garage owner said he might be interested in buying it. Give him a call—the number's on the chalkboard."

Chris stood, rooted to the spot, as man and dog climbed into the truck and drove off. When they reached the corner she closed her eyes tight in a sudden return to her senses. "Oh, darn!" She smacked her fist against her forehead. "I was going to kick him out after supper. Why did I let him go off to get his clothes?"

Chris lay perfectly still under the patterns of silver moonlight that spilled through her bedroom window. The digital clock on her round, lace-covered night table read twelve forty-five. She was thinking about her marriage . . . about pain. She had blithely hurtled herself into a marriage that had brought her more pain and anger than she'd ever thought she could endure. But she'd managed to get through it. She had cried until there were no tears left in her body . . . for her unborn daughter who would never know her father . . . for her broken dream of sharing the joys of her pregnancy with the man she loved . . . for her terrible love for a man who really didn't exist. Her husband had been vain and shallow and ruthlessly ambitious—all gilt and no substance—and she had married him. She had fallen in love with falling in love. And it had taken years before her eyes were no longer clouded with being in love. Years before she'd been able to see the man for what he was and exorcise him from her life.

A tear slid down her cheek over the loss of what might have been. Another tear gathered in the fringe of her lower lashes. It was for the empty future, and for the ache of wanting to love Ken Callahan and knowing it would never be. She was not a good judge of men—that much was clear. She couldn't trust herself to fall in love again, because this time she wouldn't be the only one hurt. This time, when the love of her life turned out to be a rat, it would be Lucy's loss as well, and no one was going to hurt Lucy like that—not if she could help it. No one was going to blithely waltz into her daughter's life, and read her books, and get her to love him, and then leave.

She sat up in bed and scrubbed the tears from her eyes,

piqued at this uncharacteristic bout with melancholia. It was all Ken Callahan's fault, barging into her life, with that unraveling grin and mouthwatering body, and stirring up feelings better left unstirred. She switched the table lamp on and immediately felt better as the room was bathed in a warm glow.

She'd decorated the room for the middle of the night. It was a room that could dispel the gloom and horror of the most terrible nightmare. It was a room that conjured up gentle sunshine and warm summer breezes. The light from the lamp reflected in the patina of her queen-sized brass bed. An ornate rolltop desk hugged one wall, it's pigeonholes overflowing with trinkets, dried flowers, bills, half-finished correspondence, and rolled-up magazines. It was framed by an assortment of pictures—pictures of trains, pictures of gorillas, pictures of ice skaters, pictures of family. The walls were the color of vanilla cream, the lush carpet a dusky rose, the down comforter covered by an apricot coverlet that matched an adjoining bath done entirely in apricot—including the walls and ceiling. Her brother had dubbed it her "sherbet phase," had merrily declared it to be sexist, and had concluded that his sister was substituting for all sorts of oral gratification.

"Probably," she'd told him breezily. "Who cares?" But deep down inside, she cared. She had made a terrible mistake, and she couldn't afford to make another. She couldn't afford the luxury of self-pity, and she couldn't admit to loneliness—not even to herself.

Pull yourself together, Chris, she fumed. Twelve forty-five. She had to be at the rink by five-twenty. She would be tired tomorrow, and it was all Ken Callahan's fault. He was sexy and charming—and a rogue. His first night under her roof, and he was off in Loudoun County, staying up to all hours and doing heaven-knows-what. It certainly didn't take five hours to gather a few clothes together. She threw the covers off and sprang out of bed. It was simple. She would go downstairs, she would make herself a cup of hot chocolate, and then she would go to sleep. And with any kind of luck, Ken Callahan would decide to stay in Loudoun County, and she'd never see him again.

She padded quietly downstairs and crept through the dark house. Reaching the kitchen, she switched on the light and set a pan of milk heating on the stove while she spooned the chocolate mix into a mug. The beginnings of a smile tipped the corners of her mouth. Her life was filled with small pleasures. Having a midnight treat in her cozy kitchen was one of them. She poured the milk into the mug and watched, enthralled, as the liquid became brown and steamy. It was her favorite mug—fine porcelain with a colorful picture of a mother gnome. Her best friend Amy had given her a set of four because she knew Chris loved gnomes. There had been no special reason for the present —Amy had simply seen them, thought of Chris, and spent her last cent on the cups. And that was the whole point, Chris reasoned. She had Amy. She had Lucy. She had Aunt Edna. What did she need with Ken Callahan?

The cocoa cooled on the counter while Chris enjoyed the quiet. The refrigerator hummed as it defrosted. The sound of suburban traffic droned in the distance. A car door slammed. A key turned in her front door. Chris felt her heart skip a beat as the front door clicked open. It was him. Damn! What rotten luck—now she was trapped in the kitchen in her nightgown. She flicked the light switch, plunging the room into darkness. Maybe he hadn't seen the light. Maybe he wasn't hungry or thirsty. She closed her eyes in silent prayer. *Let him go directly to his room.*

A broad-shouldered, slim-hipped form appeared in the middle of the doorway. His face was bathed in shadow, giving Chris no clue to his mood. His good arm rested casually against the louvered door. "Hiding?" His voice was a velvet murmur. Low and purposefully seductive.

Rational thought and good intentions flew from her mind like autumn leaves on a windy day. She was aware only of the flame flickering to life deep within her. And she was suffused with the pleasure of his presence, with the predatory purr of his voice.

"You're standing in the moonlight, Chris. Would you like to know what I see?"

Chris felt her lips part, but no words emerged. She

stood statue still, barely breathing, her heart thumping in her chest.

"I see a beautiful woman with silver curls and moonbeams spilling over ivory shoulders and the curve of her arm. All highlight and shadow and breathless expectancy." He took a step toward her. "So slender and young," he whispered in hoarse reverence. "I'd be afraid to touch you if it weren't for the shadows."

"Shadows?"

He was very close now. Close enough for her to see his eyes, black with desire. He drew the tip of his finger across her lower lip. "This shadow." He gasped as he felt her tremble under his touch. "This shadow that tells me your lips are parted, waiting to be kissed." He closed his eyes and touched his open mouth to hers. He deepened the kiss with maddening languor, his tongue coaxing, waiting, promising, before plunging deep into her mouth in undisguised hunger. When she responded, he drew away to continue the seduction.

"And this shadow at your pulse point," he murmured against her sensitized skin, each word brushing fiery paths toward the spot in her neck that throbbed in silent wanting. He lifted his head to watch her, to savor the desire written on her face. His smoldering gaze dropped to visually caress the silken skin left exposed by the low scoop neck of her nightgown, then traveled lower to her small high breasts, barely hidden beneath the soft white flannel gown. His voice was hoarse when he finally spoke. "And these shadows, Chris. Dark and swollen." His large hand gently cupped her breast while his thumb slid across her dusky nipple.

She closed her eyes and moaned softly, succumbing to the pleasure that ripped through her body at his every touch. She clasped her hands over his, pressing her turgid nipple into his palm, wanting him never to stop touching her, wanting to feel the hard length of him against her—over her. Again, Chris was treated to a searing flash of foresight, a reaffirming of what she'd sensed in the hospital: that Ken Callahan would be a careful, sensitive lover; that he would allow their desire to build until it was unbearable; and that when his passion was finally unleashed, it would be all-encompassing, devastatingly intense, and like none she had ever known.

His mouth found hers with startling urgency and his tongue plunged deep inside, seeking sweet liquids, demanding her passion to match his own. Chris leaned into him. Her breasts pressed against his muscled chest. Her lower body sought the evidence of his arousal. She kissed him without reserve, her tongue playing with his, accepting his thrusts, inviting him to explore still-untouched shadows.

"Sexy lady," he rasped. "I need you." He kissed her again, long and deep. "I need you to love me." He swung around to lift her in his arms, forgetting the day-old cast. *C-l-a-n-n-n-g!* The plaster cast smashed against an empty copper fruit bowl sitting innocently on the counter. The bowl sailed through space and clattered onto the floor. *Arrrrang arrrrang arrrrang!* The bowl whirled to a stop.

"Oh my God!" Chris choked.

"What the hell was that?"

Chris giggled and bent to retrieve the bowl. "It was a copper bowl."

Lights flashed on upstairs. A door was thrown open. "What's going on down there?" Edna yelled.

They looked at each other like two children caught pilfering the cookie jar.

Ken rested his forehead against a cabinet door. "I think I might cry."

"I think I might buy more fruit bowls."

"Saved by the bell, huh?"

Chris looked at him in the moonlight. His face was still tinged with the strain of unsated desire. "I didn't mean for this to happen," she explained in a voice that was shaky with emotion. "I couldn't sleep, and I was making myself a cup of cocoa."

"I guessed. I could smell the cocoa as soon as I opened the front door." He took the fruit bowl from her and set it back on the counter. "And I didn't mean for *this* to happen," he told her with a menacing grin aimed at the now-silent bowl.

"Yeah," Chris breathed. "I believe that."

Aunt Edna's voice rattled down the stairs. "Chris? Is that you making that racket?"

"Yes, Aunt Edna. I was making cocoa, and I accidentally knocked the fruit bowl off the counter."

"Land sakes," she grumbled, "scared the daylights out of me."

"Why don't you come down and have some cocoa with me?"

Ken shook his finger at her. "Shame on you. That's so cowardly."

"And so wise."

"A cup of cocoa," Edna repeated happily. "Don't that sound nice! I'll go get my robe."

Ken reluctantly pushed himself away from Chris. "You'll regret this as much as I will. You'll lie in bed for the rest of the evening feeling unsatisfied and wanting me, and I won't be able to come to you."

Chris shivered at the sexy timbre of his voice and the lethal calm in his eyes. She knew he was right, but she had no choice. *Thank goodness for Aunt Edna. I have no defenses against this man. I feel like a moth being drawn into the flame.*

Aunt Edna's slippered feet slapped against the stair carpet.

Ken turned and left before Edna reached the kitchen.

Chris wrapped her arms across breasts that still throbbed with desire and was consumed with an all-encompassing loneliness for Ken Callahan.

Chapter Four

CHRIS LOOKED AT the slim gold watch on her wrist and groaned. Five-ten. She was late. She was tired. She was cranky. And she certainly didn't have time for breakfast. She slung the gray sports bag over her shoulder and shuffled down the dark stairs. Ordinarily, Aunt Edna would be up making breakfast, but she'd overslept today, too. Chris shrugged into her vest and reached for the doorknob.

A large hand closed over her small one. "Making a hasty retreat?"

Chris turned and found herself squashed between the door and Ken Callahan. He smiled good morning and kissed her softly, as if she were a delicate treasure. He was right, she thought, he was a terrific kisser. She halfheartedly reminded herself that she was grouchy and didn't want to be kissed . . . or talked to . . . or smiled at. She tried to look stern. "What are you doing up so early?"

"I want to watch you teach ice skating."

Chris wrinkled her nose. "It's five-ten. It's dark out. The birds aren't even up yet. Go back to bed."

"Are you kidding? I even took a shower to do this."

"Well, I don't feel like having an audience today. I'm tired and grumpy . . . and I don't want to be bothered by you."

"Hmmmm, couldn't you sleep last night?" His tone was mockingly innocent and maddeningly triumphant.

She tilted her nose up defiantly. "I slept fine after I had my cocoa."

"I'm glad cocoa has such a soothing effect on you." He nuzzled her hair, inhaling the scent of her shampoo. "I didn't have any cocoa to soothe my frustration. I lay awake all night, thinking about you."

Chris wound her arms around his neck and murmured in contentment. "Poor Ken."

He chuckled softly and kissed her neck. "You're so responsive. So nice to love."

And dumb. And weak. And sappy. Had that been her voice murmuring "Poor Ken"? "Ugh! Get away from me." Chris pushed him away, stamping her foot in frustration. "What is it about you that turns me into mush?"

Ken sucked in his breath as her boot accidentally came down on his bare foot. He stood absolutely still for a second, his right hand holding her arm in a viselike grip. He expelled his breath and closed his eyes. The expletive that escaped between his clenched teeth caused Chris to raise her eyebrows.

"You'd better not let Aunt Edna hear you say that. She'll let you have it with the wooden spoon."

He relaxed his hand, smoothed the fingerprints from the sleeve of her warm-up suit, and regarded her with calm fury. "You broke my toe."

Chris looked down at the bloody gash and already swelling toe. "Why don't you have shoes on?" she wailed.

"Because I can't get shoes on by myself. Because you broke my damn arm. Because I haven't had a chance to buy loafers, yet."

Chris bit her lip. "Maybe it's not broken?"

"I'm sure it's broken. I'm getting good at recognizing broken bones."

"Maybe we should put some ice on it."

"I don't want ice," he ground out. "I want to go to the hospital." He lowered himself gingerly onto a stair and held out a sock. "Just help me put this damn sock on . . .

and this damn shoe. And then you can drive me to the damn hospital."

Chris glared at him and tugged the sock onto his healthy foot. She slipped his running shoe on and tied the laces. "I don't see what you're so damn mad about. It isn't as if it's entirely my fault."

"Not entirely your fault?" he sputtered. "Lady, you're a fruitcake. I suppose you think I saw your boot coming down, and I slipped my toe underneath it on purpose."

"You know perfectly well what I mean. You . . . you take advantage of me."

"Well, you're not going to have to worry about it anymore. I can't afford to break any more body parts. At this rate, I'll be a paraplegic by Friday. And God forbid what might happen if I ever got you into bed! A man would have to be crazy to take his clothes off anywhere near you."

Chris grit her teeth and held his other sock out to him. "Do you want me to put this on you?"

"Don't touch my foot!" he shouted. "Just get me a towel so I don't bleed all over my truck."

By the time she returned with the towel, he'd already hobbled out to the curb.

Chris stopped for a light and nervously cracked her knuckles. It had been a long, silent ride to the hospital. Ken slouched in the seat next to her, staring stonily straight ahead, his arms crossed in front of him. He hadn't said a word since they'd left the house, and Chris was afraid to begin conversation. What on earth do you say to a man after you've broken his toe? And his arm. Glorioski, Mr. Callahan, I'm really sorry! Chris felt tears burning behind her eyes. *Thank goodness for the darkness,* she breathed. *This is awful enough, I don't need to have him see me crying. I don't even know why I'm feeling such anguish over this whole silly episode.* She blinked back the tears and decided it must be hormones. The man was hell on hormones.

She heard him rustle in the seat beside her, and knew with a sinking heart that he was watching her. His fingertips brushed across her cheek.

"What's this for?"

Chris ignored the question. She turned into the hospital lot and cut the motor. "Would you rather I come in with you? Or should I wait here?"

"I'd rather you tell me why you're crying."

Chris stared miserably down at her warm-up jacket.

He reached over with his good arm and hauled her across the seat, onto his lap.

"Be careful! Your arm! Your toe!"

He kissed the tears on her cheek and nestled her into the crook of his arm. "Honey, when I've got you on my lap I can't even feel my arm or my toe."

Chris closed her eyes and buried her flushed face into his shoulder.

His lips feathered lingering kisses in her orange curls. "You like me, don't you?" he said in a husky whisper that sent her heart tumbling in her chest.

She couldn't speak. She was overwhelmed with a rush of conflicting emotions. She did like him. Even more horrible, she might be falling in love with him. How else to explain the lump that was becoming a permanent fixture in her throat? How else to explain the sense of dread—of impending doom—of unwanted, fingertip-tingling excitement? She nodded her head yes, and pressed her cheek against his chest.

"And you're sorry you broke my toe?"

She nodded again.

"Is there anything else?"

Chris sighed. There were about a million other things, but none she wanted to say out loud. And nothing she could coherently explain when he was kissing her hair. Warm waves of desire were washing away sensible thought. She concluded that if she stayed in his arms for another thirty seconds she would lose all control and attack him, and they'd probably be arrested for doing X-rated things in a hospital parking lot. She took a deep breath and pushed herself from his lap. "I suppose I do like you, a little," Chris admitted. "And I'm sorry about your toe, but I think we should keep this living arrangement strictly business."

"Why?"

Chris squeezed her finely arched eyebrows together into a frown. "Because I'm not too happy about having a man in my house. And I definitely don't want one in my life. I like my life just the way it is . . . was . . . before yesterday."

He regarded her with open amusement. "What a load of baloney."

"Unh!" she grunted. "You are the most exasperating man." She threw her hands into the air in frustration. "Go get your blasted toe fixed."

Ken looked at the stretch of cold macadam between the truck and the reception room. He looked down at his blue-and-purple bare foot partially wrapped in an apricot hand towel.

"Sorry," she whispered. "I wasn't thinking." She started the truck and drove to the emergency entrance where he got out and hobbled inside.

Chris parked and joined him at the front desk, where he was filling out a form. An inquisitive nurse leaned over the desk and looked at his toe. "Weren't you folks in here yesterday?"

Ken raised his white cast. "Yesterday she broke my arm," he announced merrily.

A second nurse appeared. Chris felt her face flame as the two nurses studied her suspiciously.

Ken completed the form. He raised his foot. "Today she broke my toe."

"It was an accident," Chris gasped.

The nurses looked at each other knowingly and studiously returned to their work.

"How could you embarrass me like that?" Chris looked around furtively to see if anyone else had heard.

"It's okay." He grinned. "She probably thought it was part of some bizarre sexual ritual."

"Good heavens."

Ken reached into his pocket and handed Chris a quarter. "It's time for you to call the rink now and tell them you'll be late, again."

Chris took the quarter and was struck by the unpleasant reality that she'd sent this man to the hospital two days in a row—and that if positions had been reversed, she doubted she could be so good-natured. "I suppose I should be happy you have a sense of humor," she ventured.

"Honey, my good mood has little to do with my sense of humor."

Aunt Edna's eyes opened wide as she stood back from the door. "What the devil happened?"

Ken carefully swung his foot over the doorjamb and eased himself into the room with the help of a single crutch. "It's nothing serious, Aunt Edna. I stubbed my toe in the dark this morning and broke it."

Chris slammed the door behind them. "He did not. He got fresh with me, and I stomped on it."

Ken rested on his crutch, and looked at her quizzically. "I thought you found that story embarrassing."

"Oh, what the hell," she exclaimed in an offhand huff. "So I broke it. What's the big deal?"

Ken smiled at Aunt Edna. "She's sorry she broke it."

Edna looked at the swollen toe taped to the one next to it. "He got fresh with you, huh?"

"Yes. Well, no. He sort of got me . . . disturbed."

"Hmmm," Edna said. "Disturbed?"

Ken slouched into the wingback chair and stretched his long legs in front of him, watching Chris with unguarded affection. "Disturbed?" he asked, the twitching corners of his mouth the only evidence of strangled laughter.

"I'd love to stay and explain all of this," Chris told them, "but I've got to get to the rink."

"Will you be home for lunch?" Edna asked.

Chris kissed the old woman good-bye and headed for the door. "No, I have to do some choreography today. I probably won't be back until suppertime."

Chris checked her watch as she walked up the steps to her town house. It was six-fifteen, and she felt as if she hadn't slept in days. She opened the door and sniffed. A delicious aroma of herbs and spices wafted through the house. Aunt Edna's world-famous oven-fried chicken, she decided. She flung her bag into a corner of the hall and shuffled toward the kitchen. It was after a terribly long day like this that she was especially thankful for Aunt Edna. If it weren't for Edna, Chris knew she'd be staring into the freezer right now, wondering what the heck she could shove into the microwave. If it weren't for Edna, the role of breadwinner and single mother would leave little time for Chris to read Dr. Seuss or listen attentively to Lucy's exploits in school. Chris pushed through the kitchen doors. "Aunt Edna—"

Ken turned from the stove and gave her a look like the cat who swallowed the canary. "Nope. Just me, slaving away over a hot stove."

"Where's Aunt Edna?"

"Kansas City."

"What do you mean, Kansas City?"

"Your cousin Stephanie had the baby three weeks premature and Edna flew out to stay with the twins."

"How could she do that?"

"Stephanie? I don't think she had much choice. George said her water broke at three twenty-five and she went right into labor . . . "

Chris blinked in dazed disbelief. Yesterday he'd been a stranger. Today he was ensconced in her kitchen, talking about her family as if it were his own. Babies and labor and broken water. "No," she intoned mechanically, "not Stephanie . . . Aunt Edna. How could Aunt Edna do this to me? It will take me days to find someone reliable to watch Lucy."

"Edna took Lucy with her."

"She can't do that! What about school?"

Ken took a bag of noodles from the counter and looked at it, mystified. He turned the bag over and read the instructions, his face brightening with the realization that he now knew how to cook noodles. "Edna said she'll only be gone for a week, and that Lucy could use a vacation. I don't think Edna is very impressed with first grade."

Cold panic squeezed at Chris's heart. The two people she loved most in the world were gone without even so much as a hug good-bye. And she was left alone with Ken Callahan. It was the latter condition that set her stomach churning and adrenaline flowing.

Ken reached out and gathered her to him. "You look like a lost little kitten," he cooed. He stroked her hair. "Don't worry. They'll be fine. I put them on the plane, myself. And Edna said they'd call as soon as they got to Kansas City."

"How did you get them to the airport?"

"Taxi." He raised his foot to display a bright red woolen sock covering the broken toe. "A broken toe isn't so bad."

She stepped away from him. "It was nice of you to help Edna and Lucy to the airport, but you're going to have to leave, now."

"I live here, remember?"

"I don't want you to live here."

Ken filled a pot with water and put it on the stove to boil. "Of course you do. Who will make your supper when you come home late like this?"

"You?" she snorted.

He pulled a package of frozen vegetables from the freezer and read the instructions. "I always wanted to learn how to cook." He set the vegetables aside and dumped the entire bag of noodles into the boiling water.

"Holy cow," Chris muttered. "I hope you like noodles. That could feed a family of six for two days."

He seemed undaunted. "Hmmm," he replied and emptied sixteen ounces of peas into a small saucepan. He smiled at her. "I surmise by the look of horror on your face that I'm cooking too many peas too."

"I usually measure out about half and then tie the rest of the bag up with a twister tie."

"Twister tie?"

Chris wrinkled her nose. "This isn't going to work. I don't need a cook. I think your aptitude is dubious, anyway."

"Boy, you get cranky after a hard day at the skating rink," he teased. He pushed her into the dining room and held her chair.

Chris looked at the table. Matching mauve linen tablecloth and napkins. Crystal goblets. The good china. Sterling candlestick holders and ivory tapers. Freshly polished silverware. "You've gone to a lot of trouble. It's very pretty."

"Actually, Aunt Edna did it. She wanted me to make a good impression on you."

"Hmmm."

"She likes me."

"She's not too choosy, you realize. Last week she fixed me up with the meter reader. And before that it was the butcher."

"Why is she so determined to get you married?"

"I suppose because she had a wonderful marriage, and she wants the same for me."

Ken leaned against the table and studied Chris. "Wouldn't you like a wonderful marriage?"

"I've already tried marriage. It wasn't wonderful."

"But it could be. Don't you want to give it another shot?"

"No."

"Edna told me you were a great skater because you never gave up."

"I never gave up on skating because I knew I was good. I'm not good at being married." Chris turned away from the intensity of his blue-black gaze. Why was he doing this—it wasn't like he was ready to propose or something.

"I think you'd make a great wife. You just need some practice."

"Uh-huh." Chris turned back toward him, one eyebrow raised quizzically.

"I could help you out . . . " He grinned. "You could practice on me."

"That's a very generous offer, but I think I'll pass." The sound of sputtering water turning to steam hissed from the kitchen. "The peas"—Chris gestured—"turn down the heat."

A lid clanked in the kitchen. Silence followed. "Okay," he finally called, "I give up. How the hell do you get these peas out of all this water?"

Endearing, Chris thought. Ruggedly masculine but soft on the underside. And very skillful at using his devastating smile and easy humor. She took the copper colander from the kitchen wall and placed it in the sink. "You can pour the peas in here. And then you can use the colander to drain and rinse the noodles."

He gave a light husbandly kiss. "Thanks. Any other cooking tips I should know?"

"Are you really serious about this?"

"Absolutely." He put the peas in the glass bowl Edna had left on the counter for him. He poured the steaming noodles into the colander and ran water over them. "How am I doing?"

Chris gave him a begrudging smile. He was doing fine with the noodles, and he was doing fine with his assignment of making a good impression. Ken Callahan was a man who knew how to drop back and punt. They carried the food into the dining room and took places opposite each other.

Ken looked at Edna's chicken with reverent admiration.

"I'm not sure I've ever seen a man look at a piece of chicken like that."

"I can't remember the last time I had home cooking. It seems like I've been on the road for a century." He put a pat of butter on his noodles and watched it melt. "My mother is a great cook—she makes these noodles in a cheese sauce . . ." He looked up at her with beguiling blue eyes. "Do you know how to do that? Do you suppose you could teach me to make cheese sauce?"

"There's a recipe for cheese sauce in the recipe box on the counter." She studied him intently for a minute, trying to imagine Ken Callahan as a young boy. He'd probably been spoiled rotten. What mother could say no to those big blue eyes? "Tell me about your family."

He sliced a piece of chicken and chewed it thoughtfully. "I guess I come from a large family by today's standards— one brother and three sisters. I'm the oldest, and I'm the only one unmarried. My parents still live in the same two-story frame house that I grew up in—in Pennsylvania. Nothing fancy, but lots of love and lots of noise. I have six nephews and four nieces. You can't imagine what Christmas Day sounds like."

"Does everyone come to your parents' house for Christmas?"

Ken speared another piece of chicken. "The kids enjoy getting their presents under their own Christmas trees." He savored a forkful of buttered noodles and grinned. "They were afraid Santa wouldn't know to bring their presents to my parents' house, so we designated December twenty-eighth as Family Christmas every year. It makes it easier to travel, too. My brother lives in Connecticut. My sister Maggie moved to Seattle last year. Cara lives in Cape May. My youngest sister, Erin, is the only one still in Pennsylvania. She lives about a half mile from my parents."

"Sounds like a nice family."

Ken nodded. "I don't get to see them as much as I'd like." He looked critically at the bowl still filled with peas. "Too many peas," he agreed, taking another helping. "What about you? Do your parents still live in Colorado?"

Chris shook her head. "My mom died when I was nineteen. My dad died three years ago. Heart disease."

"I'm sorry."

Chris nodded.

"You have a brother?"

"Ted. Two years older than me. He's still in Colorado." Her gaze rested on his competent hands, slicing off another bite of chicken.

"What brought you east?"

"This job," she said, turning her attention back to her own plate. "They needed someone with international experience to build a competitive skate program. It's a small rink, but it has some good skaters—last year two of my students qualified for national competition."

"You like teaching skating." He speared a final forkful of noodles.

"I love it. I find it much more satisfying than competing. And much less painful."

Ken looked at his empty plate with a contented sigh. "And I find cooking much more satisfying than construction work."

Chris laughed softly. "What you find satisfying is eating . . . not cooking."

He raised his eyes, suddenly filled with a hunger that had nothing to do with peas or oven-fried chicken. When he spoke his voice rubbed against Chris like velvet on silken skin. "I have something special planned for dessert."

Chris felt her temperature rise and wondered how he did it. With a single teasing sentence and one semismoldering look, he had instantly turned her into a quivering mass of overheated half-wit. She narrowed her eyes and hoped she looked menacing. "You looking to get something else broken?"

Ken raised his hands in mock self-defense. His eyes softened with the recognition of her panic. "You don't like dessert?" he asked in exaggerated innocence.

She shook her finger at him. "You weren't talking about dessert."

He began stacking the dishes. "I was going to suggest Irish coffee in front of a roaring fire, and"—he disappeared behind the kitchen door—"a plate full of goodies." He reappeared with a bakery bag and a sterling plate covered with a paper doily. "I stopped at a bakery on the way home from the airport. You fix the cookies, and I'll make coffee. I may not be much of a cook, but I make an excellent Irish coffee."

Chris stared at the white bag. It was from her favorite bakery. She peeked inside. All her favorite cookies—and Linzer tortes. She loved Linzer tortes. Smells like a plot, she thought. This could only be Aunt Edna's work. The heavenly aroma of coffee brewing drifted into the dining room. Chris sniffed in appreciation and arranged the cookies on the silver plate. A doily. She sighed. Edna was really going all out on this one.

"Chris," Ken called. "I need help. I can't carry two mugs of hot coffee with only one hand."

Chris placed the cookies and the coffee on a tray and followed Ken downstairs. There was already a fire glowing in the fireplace. An electric thrill raced through Chris as she watched Ken add a log and stoke the embers into life. He wore a powder-blue rugby shirt with the left sleeve cut at the elbow. His silky black hair curled over the white cotton collar, the muscles in his back rippled as he moved, and his biceps bulged under the soft fabric. Chris allowed herself the intoxicating pleasure of admiring the broad shoulders and slim hips. His shirt hung loose over clean, faded jeans that were loose enough to be comfortable, but tight enough to display well-defined quadriceps and a perfect backside. *I'd trade every Linzer torte on this plate for one nibble at that perfect behind,* she decided, and was immediately horrified that she'd even thought such a thing. She felt her face flame.

He rose from the fire and regarded her with amused curiosity. "Are you flushed from the fire, or have you been thinking naughty thoughts?"

Chris put her hands to her burning cheeks. "This is embarrassing."

He settled beside her on the big overstuffed couch and rested his injured foot on the coffee table, chuckling softly at her discomfort. "Here"—he offered Chris half of his sugar cookie—"take a bite. It will be so exquisite you'll forget about being embarrassed."

Chris bit into the cookie and let it melt in her mouth, ruefully thinking it would take more than a cookie to overcome her undeniable reaction to his heady presence. Sexy. She tried taking slow, deep, regular breaths, but her heart was still pounding.

"Edna told me about this bakery. She said it was your favorite—I can see why." He waved his half-eaten piece of cookie at her. "I'm an expert on cookies, and these are definitely top of the line."

Chris licked at the dollop of whipped cream floating on the top of her coffee. His honesty was unnerving. He made no pretense about Edna's help in all this, and he made it perfectly clear that he was on his best behavior, trying to make a good impression. Chris wondered about his intentions. He obviously wanted to live in her house. She wasn't sure why, except that he really did seem to miss being part of a family. And he was physically attracted to her. That was unmistakable. And mutual. No man had ever affected her quite like Ken Callahan—not even Steven.

Chris watched him under lowered lashes and felt the warmth flood through her. It was a bittersweet feeling, lovely and sensual as a cat by a heated hearth, and sad because it was all so impossible. *I don't want another man in my life,* she repeated to herself. *Especially this one. He's much too handsome. Too virile. He probably collects women like ants at a picnic.* But she had to admit this was very nice.

They sat side by side on the comfortable couch, eating Linzer tortes in silence, listening to the hiss and crackle of the fire. Chris sipped at the coffee. She curled her legs under her and closed her eyes drowsily. "It's been such a long day," she mumbled in halfhearted apology. "I can't keep my eyes open."

Chapter Five

"COME ON, SLEEPYHEAD." Ken's voice was as gentle as the hand that stroked her cheek. "Time to get up."

Chris blinked in the darkness, trying to organize the confusion of her mind.

Ken smiled at her. It was an irresistible, devastating grin—even at the crack of dawn. His white teeth flashed in his black beard, reminding Chris of a pirate. "You fell asleep right in the middle of your Linzer torte last night," he said with a trace of laughter. "You mumbled something about it being a long day and then you were gone."

"Did Edna call?"

"Yes. Everyone is fine. You should call Kansas later this morning. Lucy lost a tooth somewhere over Wheeling, West Virginia. I think she'd like to brag to you about it."

A shaft of golden light escaped from his open bedroom door, partially illuminating the rec room. Chris gazed sleepily at the man sitting beside her. She unconsciously reached out and touched a lock of black hair that was still wet from his shower. "You smell nice. Warm and spicy . . . like men's soap and mint toothpaste."

He captured her hand and pressed a lingering kiss against the inside of her wrist. His eyes held her. "Be careful. It wouldn't take much to get me under that quilt with you."

Chris felt her heart jump at the touch of his lips. *It wouldn't take much for me to drag you under here,* she silently groaned. "I ...uh...I was just..." She closed her eyes tight. "Oh damn. You've got me stuttering."

"Mmmm, I seem to have a strange effect on you."

"Yeah. An annoying mixture of lust and sheer panic, and I intend to ignore both of them." She stretched under the down quilt. "I see you tucked me in."

"I considered undressing you and putting you to bed, but I didn't want to risk another broken body part. I need all the parts I have left."

"Very wise." She sat up and rubbed her eyes. "What time is it?"

"Four-thirty. Better get moving. Breakfast will be served in twenty minutes."

She looked at him warily. "Are you cooking breakfast?"

"Edna told me you have orange juice, coffee, and an egg over easy."

Chris shook her head and muttered to herself as she climbed the stairs. "The woman even told him what I have for breakfast. Heaven only knows what else she told him. He probably knows my shoe size and my cholesterol level."

Chris locked her bedroom door and her bathroom door and still felt uncomfortable when she stripped for her shower. There was no escaping Ken Callahan. He had invaded her bastion of female tranquility and security. He permeated every part of the house. He stirred every latent sex-related hormone in her body. She lathered her shoulders and watched the soap cascade in slippery rivulets over the swell of high firm breasts and rosy nipples. She was suddenly glad she had kept herself in shape. Thank goodness I inherited a healthy metabolism and a naturally slim body from my mother, she thought. Her hectic schedule didn't leave time for fancy spas and racquetball dates. She exercised daily with the skaters in a general conditioning class and tried to run at least six miles a week. She examined herself more closely. Her waist was still small and supple. Her stomach was flat. Her legs still showed good muscle definition in the quadriceps and calves. Not an ounce of fat, she concluded with great satisfaction. She ducked her head under the steaming water and poured shampoo into the tangle of orange curls.

Of course, she assured herself, the fact that she was taking an appraisal of her body for the first time in seven years had nothing to do with Ken Callahan. She simply had a little extra time this morning and had happened to notice she was still trim and desirable. In fact, she had so much time she decided to use the expensive herbal rinse that made her hair shiny and soft to touch. She whisked out of the shower, humming happily, towel-dried her hair, and smoothed moisturizer over her flawless complexion.

The warm-up suits neatly folded in her dresser drawer seemed strangely bland. They were comfortable and sensible . . . and blah. Mostly gray. Not today, she decided. She didn't feel gray. She felt red. Maybe turquoise. And she didn't feel a bit baggy. She rummaged through her bottom drawer, finally finding a black Lycra skintight body suit with stirrup feet. She ripped the tags off a brand-new, sparkling-white turtleneck and pulled it over her head and added a black sweater with bright blue-and-white racing stripes running the length of the arm. A quick look in the mirror brought a smile to her lips as she settled the wide ribbing on her hips. She carefully added a touch of blue shadow, swiped at her lashes with the mascara wand, and was startled to find that her cheeks were glowing pink without blusher. "Goodness," she giggled. "Must have been the hot shower."

Chris flew down the stairs and pushed through the kitchen door. A pregnant silence filled the small room. There was a peculiar expression on Ken's face as he stood by the stove. He seemed poised on the brink of some emotion—a look of general horror about him; his eyes wide with surprise, his mouth twitching with what might be laughter, his black brows drawn together in consternation. Chris stopped still in her tracks. She followed his eyes to a spot on the floor just inches from her feet. Her first reaction was to classify the object on the floor with snakes, spiders, mice, and unidentified slime. She jumped back a foot and screamed. "Eeeeeh! What is it?" When it didn't move she bent down to take a closer look and realized it was an egg. Perfectly fried. Over easy.

"It's an egg," he said tonelessly. "Over easy. Just the way you like it."

"You did a good job," Chris told him, almost choking. "It's perfect. Except . . ."—she swallowed hard—"except it's on the floor."

"The little devil slid out of the pan."

Chris clapped her hands over her mouth in an attempt to abort the gales of laughter that were rising in her throat.

Ken bent over the egg with her. "You may as well go ahead and laugh. You look like you're ready to burst an eardrum from internal pressure."

"I'm sorry," she gasped between spasms of hysteria. "I really am sorry."

"It's the first egg I've ever cooked . . . in my entire life." He slid the spatula under the egg and lifted it from the linoleum. "I think it's dead."

Chris stood ramrod straight, saluted the egg, and tooted out taps.

Ken gave her a withering look and dumped the mess into the garbage disposal. "Would you like me to try again?"

"No. I think I'll pass on the egg today." She swallowed her juice and sipped at the coffee. "Mmmm. You do make excellent coffee."

Ken lounged against the wall, watching her with an intensity that made her feel as if she were melting inch by inch. Slowly and hungrily, his eyes traveled the length of her. "Do you have any idea what you look like? Does Aunt Edna let you go out dressed like that?"

Chris bit back a smile. Damn right she knew what she looked like—sexy as all get-out. And Edna would do cartwheels to get her to dress like this. Edna hated the warm-up suits. Edna called them camouflage.

Chris feigned innocence. "What's wrong with this?"

"It's . . . slinky." His face clouded. "Beautiful soft orange curls and eyes like a young lioness . . . and now this outfit." He reached out and ran his finger along the outside of her thigh. "It's silky," he noted, molding his hand to her hipbone. "It fits you like skin. What on earth is this? Something special for skaters?"

"It's a body suit. A unitard."

He peeked under her sweater with more curiosity than passion. "It goes all the way up."

Chris slapped at his hand. "Don't do that!"

He smoothed the ribbing back over her hips. His eyes softened until Chris thought he looked like a blue-eyed cocker spaniel. "You're such an enigma, Chris Nelson. Flushed cheeks and soft lips and a little breathless. When you direct all that wide-eyed excitement at me it turns my stomach upside down." He cupped her chin in his hand and rubbed his thumb lightly across her lower lip. "I've fallen in love with you, and I'm worried because you're sending me such a mixture of signals. Sometimes I think you're beginning to like me, and then all of a sudden panic sets in and you get all bristly."

Fallen in love with her! Chris felt as if someone were squeezing the air from her lungs. "I don't want you to fall in love with me," she gasped. "And I certainly don't want to fall in love with you."

"What's wrong with me?"

Chris found herself smiling at his injured tone. "Nothing's wrong with you. That's the problem . . . you're perfect. You're attractive and sensitive and fun to be with. I could easily fall in love with you . . . if I wanted to fall in love."

Ken plunged his hands into his pockets and studied her. "You don't want to fall in love?"

Chris turned away from him and nervously smoothed an imaginary wrinkle in her sweater. Of course she wanted to fall in love. Everyone wanted to fall in love. Real love must be wonderful. But fake love is awful . . . and she obviously wasn't capable of telling the difference. She'd thought Steven had loved her. What a laugh. She folded her hands in front of her to keep from fiddling with the sweater. "I can't fall in love," she told him quietly.

"Why not?"

"It's too painful." She heard her voice falter and took a deep breath to pull herself together. "I have a very nice life. I don't have any intention of complicating it with an emotionally draining relationship."

Ken crossed his arms over his chest and studied her. "I can understand how you feel. You've had a terrible experience, and you're afraid to let yourself love again. But it's wrong for you to judge me by the asinine behavior of another man."

Chris turned and faced him. "Right or wrong has nothing to do with it. It's simply survival and motherly instincts and my own personal limitations. I'm not ready to open myself up that much to someone again. I may never be ready."

Chris lowered her eyes and inspected her shoe. The ensuing silence seemed thick with tension and bitter thoughts. Finally Ken cleared his throat, and she looked up.

His eyes sparkled with mischief. "So, you don't want to get married, and you don't want to fall in love. How do you feel about casual sex?"

Chris felt a grudging smile tug at the corners of her mouth. "I don't do casual sex."

Ken slid his hand to her waist and drew her to him, burying his face in her curly hair. His lips were warm, and soft and coaxing. His tongue teased lightly over hers. She felt him savor the kiss as if it were a forbidden and rare delicacy, and her heart responded to the compliment with an aching desire for more. They parted slowly, watching each other dreamily, delighting in the sensual intimacy that lingered. Chris felt him withdraw. A look of questioning uncertainty flickered in his blue eyes for just a moment and was replaced with resolute calmness. Then he sighed and held her at arm's length. "If you don't want to fall in love, and you don't want to have meaningless sex . . . what the hell is this that's happening between us?"

Chris bit her lower lip. "It's a total lack of willpower. There's something about you that turns me into mindless overheated mush."

"Mindless overheated mush? Is that anything like gruel? Or Quaker Oats?"

Chris threw her hands into the air. "It isn't funny. I hate it—and it's all your fault. No one else has ever done this to me; you have some horrible effect on my hormones."

His eyes opened wide in pleased surprise. A smile twitched over his mouth. "Really?" he said, gloating. "How terrible!"

Chris observed his unabashed glee with embarrassed fury. "And you should be ashamed of yourself. Here you are taking advantage of my . . . affliction."

He grinned at her in silent amazement. "Affliction? If I thought you were serious I'd really be mad."

"I am serious," she snapped, more out of momentum than seriousness.

He held the curve of her jaw in his hand. "You're a healthy, sensuous, responsive woman. That's a beautiful gift, not an affliction. And you're wrong about my taking advantage of the situation. I don't want you doing something you'll regret just because I stir up your hormones." He tapped her temple with his index finger. "When I take you to bed it will be all of you. Your lovely illogical mind included." He spun her around and pushed her toward the front door. "We'll talk about this more over dinner. If you don't hurry, you'll be late for work."

Chris checked her watch and grimaced—she had no time in her schedule for knee-weakening kisses or men falling in love.

Ken reached into the hall closet and extracted Chris's ski jacket. "It's supposed to be cold today—maybe some snow," he told Chris, zipping her into the coat as if she were going off to kindergarten. "Be careful driving home." He gave her a slow, lingering kiss and playfully swatted her behind as she swung through the door.

She turned with an indignant profanity on the tip of her tongue, decided that a simple pat on the backside didn't warrant that much hostility, pressed her lips together in fury, and hurried to the truck. After all, she admitted, she was mad at Chris Nelson, not Ken Callahan. Ken Callahan hadn't actually done anything wrong . . . darn it.

Bitsy leaned against the rink guardrail and smiled at Chris. "You look like you have a lot on your mind."

"Mmmmmm."

"I can't tell if you're depressed or elated. You have the most peculiar expression on your face."

"Then it registers my mood perfectly."

"A man?"

"Mmmmmm."

A devilish grin spread across Bitsy's face. "The man in the truck?"

"Yeah," Chris sighed. "Did I tell you he's living with me?"

Bitsy's eyes widened. "Fast work!"

Chris wrinkled her nose. "No. It's nothing like that. Well, it is sort of . . . oh hell! Aunt Edna rented him the downstairs of the house."

Bitsy tipped her head back and bellowed out a laugh. "Good old Aunt Edna. Somehow, I'm not surprised."

"That's not even the worst of it. My cousin Stephanie went into labor yesterday, and Edna flew off to Kansas City to help out with the twins. And she took Lucy with her."

Bitsy looked more interested by the second. "So it's just the two of you in the house?" She giggled.

"You can stop thinking whatever you're thinking. Nothing happened."

"You sound disappointed."

Chris slouched against the barrier. "I don't know. He's really yummy, but I've finally gotten over that stinker, Steven. I don't want to let another man into my life. My life is calm and orderly, now. It's comfortable." Chris screwed up her face for emphasis. "It's been over seven years since I've been really intimate with a man, and I haven't missed it . . . until Ken Callahan arrived on the scene. Now it's like an obsession. An enormous all-consuming blot on my life. Three days ago I didn't know this man existed, and now he's all I think about. I can't get near him without coming unglued. I do everything but drool." She touched her hands to her cheek. "Look at me. I get hot flashes just thinking about him."

"Wow."

"And if that isn't bad enough . . . I even like him."

Bitsy looked horrified. "I think you've slipped a cog somewhere."

"My cogs are fine." Chris bent to adjust one of her skate laces, then straightened with a sigh. "I just don't want to complicate my life. I have my work and Lucy and Edna; I don't have the time or the energy for a love affair. And I'm a terrible judge of men—what if he turns out to be another Steven Black?"

Bitsy fixed her with a direct, steady gaze. "There's only one Steven Black."

It was true, Chris admitted as she parked the truck in front of her townhouse that evening. There was only one Steven Black, and it wasn't fair to judge Ken by Steven's failings. She sat for a moment watching the promised snow sift down in giant flakes and melt on the hood of the truck. It clung tentatively to the already frozen lawn and cement sidewalk. The front porch light had been turned on to welcome her home, and soft lights glowed behind the drawn living room curtains. A small thrill of happiness fluttered through her stomach at the cozy scene. Her armor was definitely slipping. She'd do better to overlook the homey welcome and conjure images of virile spiders waiting for naive flies instead . . .

The sharp whine of a siren pierced the stillness, and Chris quirked an eyebrow. The smoke detector! She bolted to her front door and flung it open, only to be met by a cloud of gray smoke that stung her eyes and choked in her throat. "Ken!"

"I'm in the damn kitchen," he shouted over the din of the smoke detector.

"Are you okay? Should I call the fire department?"

"I can't figure out how to get this blasted alarm to shut off."

Chris made her way to the kitchen, climbed up on a chair and pressed the silencer button on the smoke detector.

From her elevated position she took a quick survey of the room. Everything seemed to be in order—with the exception of a charred lump of what she assumed used to be meat, sitting in a blackened pot in the sink.

Ken scowled up at her. "Well?" he demanded, feet set wide, hands on hips.

"Well, what?" Chris giggled.

At the sound of her laughter he shifted from his pugnacious stance. An embarrassed grin stole across his mouth. "I burned supper."

"I noticed." She stepped down and peered onto the sink. "What did it used to be?"

"Rump roast. See," he pointed out, "those small black lumps are carrots."

Chris stuck a fork into the meat but couldn't pry the blackened roast from the bottom of the pot. "What happened?"

"I had some business calls to make. And then I took a shower..."

"You have to make sure there's always a little liquid in the bottom."

"The book didn't tell me that."

Chris wiped a smudge of soot from his cheek. His eyes locked into hers at the touch of her fingertip. A silent message passed between them with tender ferocity. "Damn," Chris swore under her breath.

"Mindless mush?"

"Something like that."

"If it's any consolation, you don't do much for my powers of concentration, either."

Chris retreated, putting some physical distance between them. "I don't think it's salvageable," she said, turning her attention to the roast.

"I'll take you out to dinner."

She considered the idea for a moment, wondering how to remind him tactfully that he had no job and probably shouldn't be squandering his money. "I have a better idea. Why don't we stay home, and I'll teach you how to make macaroni and cheese?"

His face brightened. "I love macaroni and cheese."

Chris couldn't help smiling with him. "I know." *This is hopeless,* she thought, *how could anybody resist a man who made you feel like a million dollars just because you offered to make macaroni and cheese?* Sighing in resignation, Chris shrugged out of her coat. Ken took it from her and headed toward the front hall closet as she began pulling things from the refrigerator. "Milk, butter, cheddar cheese," she mumbled as she set the food on the countertop. As Ken walked back into the kitchen, she handed him the block of cheese. "You can grate this in the food processor."

His face looked blank. "Food processor?"

Chris moved the machine to the front of the counter. "Cut the cheese into chunks . . . like this. Drop them into the attachment . . . here. Press the proper button—this one —and presto!" The machine whirred.

"I think I can handle that."

Chris melted butter in a small saucepan and added a little flour, stirring with a wire whisk. "You see," she said, "two tablespoons melted butter and two tablespoons of flour."

"Hmmmm," he hummed into her hair as he watched over her shoulder.

"Then, after you've cooked this together for a minute or two, you add a cup of milk."

"Cup of milk," he repeated, the husky words vibrating along the edge of Chris's ear.

Chris closed her eyes and swallowed. "Have you grated that cheese, yet?"

"I was watching you."

"Well, you don't have to watch me anymore. That's all there is to the sauce. Now it just gets cooked until it thickens a little." Chris set a pot of water on the stove to boil.

"Grated cheese and elbow macaroni," Ken said, placing them next to the stove. "I feel like I'm assisting at surgery."

"This is nothing. Wait until I teach you how to make soup, and you have to cut up a billion vegetables."

"I'm good at vegetables. I made a salad," he said

proudly. He took a large plastic wrapped bowl from the refrigerator for her inspection.

Chris looked at his handiwork with genuine admiration. He definitely had a flair for salad.

"I noticed a hambone in here," he called over his shoulder as he rummaged in the refrigerator. "Maybe we could slice some ham off it and add it to the macaroni and cheese."

They worked together in companionable silence, setting the table, then adding cheese to the white sauce before combining it with the cooked macaroni and slivers of ham. Chris sprinkled extra cheese over the top and slid the dish into the oven to brown. They stood at the stove in hushed expectancy, waiting for their supper.

Ken grinned down at her. "I guess it's kind of dumb, but I really am enjoying myself. It's nice to work in the kitchen with you."

Chris nodded in agreement. "I like to cook, but I almost never get the chance. I never get home before six, and Lucy can't wait much longer than that to eat." She stole a slice of radish from the salad and carried the bowl into the dining room. "Besides, when Aunt Edna's here, she really isn't too crazy about me invading her kitchen." Chris took the steaming casserole from the oven and set it on the table.

Ken waved his fork at the heaping portion of macaroni he had doled out onto his plate. "I can make this, now: two tablespoons butter, two tablespoons flour, one cup of milk, and a bunch of cheese."

"Is it okay?"

"It's great."

Chris stared across the table at him. "I see you've decided to grow a beard."

Ken rubbed the black four-day-old whiskers with his thumb. "I thought I'd give it a try. What do you think?"

The thought of Ken Callahan in full beard gave her the shivers. It would be like black silk—making his sensuous smile even more enigmatic, joining the lush curls that partially hid his ears, highlighting eyes that were already far too expressive. An unbidden warmth spread through her loins at the tactile possibilities of a bearded Callahan.

Ken looked at her expectantly, waiting for an answer. "Well?"

Chris took a deep breath. "It makes you look a little . . . ah . . . primitive."

"Primitive?"

Chris toyed with her noodles. "You know . . . sort of . . ."

He was watching her closely, fork poised in midair, brows raised in question.

Chris rolled her eyes from side to side and flipped her hands palm up in a gesture of exasperation. "Well, hell. Sexy. If you must know, the damn thing makes you look incredibly sexy."

"Incredibly sexy?" His eyes opened wide. The corners of his mouth curled up in candid delight. "Damn!"

Chris couldn't keep herself from laughing. It had been an awkward admission for her to make, but he responded with such surprised happiness that she was glad she'd told him. She liked seeing him happy. And she was relieved to know that he hadn't grown it because he knew it was sexy.

"The only other times I've grown a beard have been on camping and fishing trips, and my all-male companions would hardly tell me it was sexy." He searched the salad bowl for errant chunks of broccoli. "I've always had to shave the darn thing off at the first sign of civilization." He rested his cast on the table. "Sometimes I wonder what it would be like to make love behind a beard. Would I be able to arouse my partner to new heights of sensual ecstasy?" His voice grew low and seductive, rubbing erotically against her disintegrating composure. He held her gaze with provocative, teasing eyes.

Chris swallowed against a rising tide of desire and turmoil. Her breath was shallow between slightly parted lips.

"Have you ever made love to a man with a beard?" Ken asked, his voice velvety and suggestive.

"Uh . . . no," she gasped. Her fork slid from her fingers and clattered onto her plate, causing her to jump in her seat.

Ken leaned back in his chair. A small frown drew his black brows together. "I've done it again. I've sent you into a state of total panic." He pushed his plate aside and leaned forward, elbows on the table. "After you left this morning, I sat down and made up a plan . . . which I have now screwed up. I thought I'd be on my good behavior for the next two days. Make sure everything stayed platonic so we could get to know each other better." The contrite tone left his voice, and his eyes sparkled with mischief. "And then by the weekend you'd see what a great guy I was and jump into my bed."

Chris opened her eyes wide and wrinkled her nose. "That's disgusting."

"It's not disgusting. It's human nature. I'm a perfectly healthy, sexually average male . . ."

Chris opened her eyes even wider. Healthy, yes. Sexually average, never.

". . . and my life has been crazy ever since I met you. For three days now I've walked around in a constant state of . . . ah . . . arousal. In the beginning, I didn't know why I was so attracted to you. It was just one of those things that happens . . . like catching a cold. You don't know how you got the damn thing, but it's obvious you're gonna be stuck with it until it runs its course. Now I find out that not only do you drive me crazy, but I like you. I like the way your face glows when you talk about Lucy. I like the way you wrinkle your nose and open your eyes wide, and that you laugh easily. I even like the way you get mad when you're cornered. You're a lot like me. We sputter and stomp and before you know it there's no more anger. I like your bravery and your strength and the fact that you try to make the best of any situation."

He paused and let his face relax into a satisfied smile. "And I love your macaroni and cheese." He covered her hand with his, sending a thrill racing up her arm. "Honey, you have to understand that this is hard for me, too. I've never felt like this about a woman before. I'm not exactly sure how to handle it. Last time I can remember having this little control over myself was in seventh grade."

"Seventh grade?"

"I was precocious," he bragged. "And I thought I was in love with Mary Ann Malinowski."

Chris rose and stacked the plates. "But now you know you weren't in love?"

"I was in seventh-grade lust. And I was incredibly impressed with myself. The only permanent result of it all was a seventh-grade average that matched Mary Ann Malinowski's IQ. I would have been better off if my average had matched her chest measurement."

Chris was beginning to hate Mary Ann Malinowski. "That big, huh?"

"She was known as 'the Wondergirl.'"

"Were there other girls after Mary Ann that you thought you were in love with?"

Ken carried the almost-empty casserole into the kitchen. He lounged against the sink and looked thoughtful. "There were girls that I found very attractive. There were girls that I regarded as very good friends." He shook his head. "No. There's been an unusually large gap between the great love affairs of my life." He measured coffee into the coffee maker. "I used to think it was a matter of time. While I was in school I was always scrambling for grades. I was the first person in my family to get a college diploma. My father was determined to see me graduate, and I wouldn't have disappointed him for anything." Ken grinned. "But it was tough. I'm not exactly the brainy type. I studied until two in the morning, and I still couldn't get the hang of French. I failed courses, and I made them up in summer school. I graduated five hundred sixty-seventh out of a class of six hundred and twelve."

A college degree. That was something Chris hadn't suspected. "A carpenter with a college degree?"

"After college, I got fired from fourteen jobs. I was not your ideal employee. I couldn't stand sitting indoors at a desk. And I felt strangled in a tie. Finally, I said the hell with it all and started working as a carpenter. And here I am. I don't do much carpentry work, anymore, but I'm still in construction." He took the freshly brewed coffee and put it on a tray. "I used to think that all these years I'd been too busy to fall in love. Now I think that the right person just never came along." He playfully tugged at an orange curl. "I'm busier than I've ever been, and I'm hopelessly in love with you."

"You thought you were hopelessly in love with Mary Ann Malinowski."

"True. But you don't have the . . . attributes . . . she had," he chuckled. "This time it must really be love."

Chris sniffed indignantly. "There's nothing wrong with my . . . attributes."

He looked at her longingly. "You have beautiful attributes, but If I'm going to stick to my plan I'd rather not think about them."

"Maybe your plan isn't so bad." Chris added two ceramic mugs to the coffee tray. She looked into his clear blue eyes and felt a warm rush of pleasure at the affection she saw there. She hated to admit it, but it was nice having Ken Callahan around. And it was nice having a man look at her like that. "I'd like to know you better."

He leaned forward and kissed her very softly. He drew away with no attempt to deepen the kiss. His eyes prolonged the moment with a silent, visual caress that lingered on her lips.

Chris thought about the second part of his plan. The part about jumping into his bed, and she wondered how she would ever last until Saturday.

Ken sighed. "I'm not even going to attempt a guess at what that smile means."

"Maybe we should take our coffee downstairs."

Chapter Six

KEN LEANED FORWARD in concentration, his right hand hovering over his queen. Finally, solemnly, he moved the antique ivory carving. "Check. Checkmate," he concluded.

Chris pressed her lips together in irritation. For the last two nights he'd beaten her consistently at chess, cribbage, Scrabble, two-handed pinochle, hangman, and Monopoly. Monopoly was the worst. He'd immediately landed on Boardwalk and Park Place, built hotels on all his property, and bankrupted her with such enthusiasm that it sent chills down her spine at the thought of him turned loose on corporate America. At least he wasn't patronizing, she concluded morosely, trying to find something positive in her latest defeat.

Ken moved the chess board from the couch to the coffee table. He glanced at his watch. "It's ten-thirty. You must be tired."

"A little, but it's Friday and I can sleep later tomorrow."

"Do you teach on Saturday?"

"I have a few lessons during the public skating session. And then there are patch and freestyle sessions from four to seven."

"About this patch and freestyle . . ."

"Umm?"

"What is it?"

"That's when the competitive skaters practice."

Ken stretched his long legs in front of him as he sank back into a corner of the couch. "I figured. And I know that 'patch' refers to compulsory figures, but I'm not sure why it's called patch."

"The rink is divided up into twenty-two sections. If you look closely you'll see numbers printed on the barrier that encircles the ice. A skater can buy one of those sections and then it's their private 'patch of ice' to practice figures on. At five-twenty the rink opens with a patch session. At six-oh-five it switches over to a forty-five-minute freestyle session. At the end of the freestyle session they make new ice so there can be another patch session. You always need clean ice for patch because the skaters must be able to see their tracings."

"Ice skating is a strange sport."

"I always thought football was a strange sport."

"Point taken."

Chris curled her legs under her and watched Ken Callahan. His eyes were turned toward the fire flickering in the fireplace. His lean, hard-muscled body reclined along the contours of the couch, reminding her of a powerful jungle cat enjoying the warmth of the sun. His glossy black hair curled over his ears and joined the close-cropped beard. His chest rose and fell slowly under a soft red plaid flannel shirt. He had learned to cook eggs, roast chicken, and bake brownies—just for her. He had kept the house neat, thoughtfully turned the porch light on to welcome her home each evening, and kept her mind occupied with games played in front of a roaring fire every night after dinner. He had followed the plan and allowed her some space to get to know him without sexual involvement. But the sexual involvement was always there. The extraordinary attraction they felt for each other constantly simmered below the surface. There were unguarded moments when raw hunger flared across Ken's face and her own skin burned with the desire to mold itself against his hard body —and he would ease the tension with gentle teasing. "Think you can make it to Saturday?" he'd taunt. Chris would assume a haughty look and tip her nose into the air.

"I don't know what you mean." And then they would both relax into smiles and chuckles.

Chris bit her lip as she studied Ken. Saturday was an hour and a half away. Her stomach churned at the thought. Nothing had changed in the past two days. If anything, it had gotten worse. She was falling in love. Hopelessly, deeply in love. Every instinct she possessed told her it was a terrible mistake, but she felt powerless to control the direction of her emotions. Just when she needed to be levelheaded and logical, she found herself once again blinded by love.

Everything about Ken Callahan seemed perfect. Even his mistakes. She cringed as she admitted to herself that she'd actually thought it was adorable when he somehow lost a pot holder in a caldron of spaghetti sauce and didn't discover it until it had been cooked into oblivion. How could she possibly trust herself to assess his character when she could think of nothing but his dark, unfathomable eyes and terrific tush? Shame on me, she giggled.

Ken opened his eyes and focused them on Chris. "Honey, that was such a naughty giggle."

"It sort of slipped out by mistake."

He looked at his watch. "Practicing for Saturday? You only have an hour and a half left."

The churning in her stomach increased. Dessert rose to the middle of her throat and sat waiting for further instructions. She felt beads of cold sweat break out on her upper lip. "I'm going to be sick."

Ken sat up. "Are you serious?"

She nodded, covering her mouth with a shaky hand, hoping to ward off nausea.

"That's impossible. You looked so healthy just a minute ago."

"I have spent the better part of my life throwing up." Her voice was shaky. "I have thrown up in every ice rink in the country . . . and some in Europe and Canada. I have even thrown up in Japan. Take my word for it . . . I'm going to throw up."

"Dammit! It was the spaghetti sauce. I knew we shouldn't have eaten it." He leaned forward and touched her cheek. "Chris, I'm really sorry. Honestly, I don't know how that pot holder got into it."

"It's not food poisoning—it's nerves. I always throw up when I get nervous. That's why I was so relieved to quit skating; I could never get used to performing."

"Nerves?" His face showed a mixture of concern and amazement.

"You! Saturday," she choked, running toward his bathroom. She slammed the door behind her and locked it. She sat on the cold tile floor and rested her forehead against the porcelain tub.

Ken knocked at the door. "Chris?"

"Go away."

"Open the door!"

"I'd sooner die."

"Open the door."

"I look awful when I throw up. My nose runs and my eyes get all red and watery."

"I don't care how you look, you idiot. Just open the damn door."

Chris crawled over to the bowl and opened the lid. "I can't," she croaked. "I'm going to be sick!"

The wet towel felt good against her flushed face. She'd seen the last of dessert and the last of the spaghetti, and she felt a little better. Ken supported her back with his cast-clad arm. He handed her a fresh washcloth. "Are you okay?" he asked gently.

She nodded. "This is so embarrassing."

"It's a little embarrassing for me, too. This is the first time anyone's ever thrown up over the prospect of going to bed with me."

Chris raised her eyes to his. "I'd like to make some witty retort, but I'm too sick."

He pushed the hair from her sweat-slicked forehead. "Do you always run a fever when you get nervous?"

Chris tried to stand. She held onto the sink and swayed dizzily. "Oh boy."

He scooped her into his arms, cursed the awkwardness

of the cast, and sidled through the bathroom door with her. "I think we should get you into bed."

She rested her head against his broad shoulder. "Jump back, Jack. I still have another hour."

His voice rumbled against her as he carried her up the stairs. "I'll add that to my list of your many attractive features. Attractive feature number thirty-two: can ward off lecherous men while nauseous." He squeezed her a little and kissed the top of her head. "It will come in handy when you're pregnant, again."

"Pregnant again?" She thought her voice sounded small and very far away, and she was glad she was too sick to get jittery over his implication.

He flicked the light switch, bathing her bedroom in warm shades of pink and apricot. "Pregnant, again," he repeated as he lay her down on the bed. "Don't you want to have a larger family? I had the distinct impression you enjoyed motherhood."

She looked at him through hazy, feverish eyes. "Are you going to make me pregnant?"

He sat at the edge of the bed and removed her shoes. "Only if you want me to," he told her softly. "When we're happily married, and you're sure it's the right thing."

"Happily married. The very idea gives me a headache." Chris touched her temple with her fingertips. "I feel awful."

"My official diagnosis is flu." He rummaged through her drawers and returned to the bed with a football jersey—style nightgown emblazoned with the Redskins emblem. "This looks like it would be comfortable to throw up in." He unbuttoned the flannel shirt she was wearing and eased it over her shoulders, groaning when he saw she wasn't wearing a bra. "I'm making a monumental effort to keep my eyes above your neck," he told her as he tugged the nightshirt over her head. "I hope you appreciate my gentlemanly effort."

"I appreciate your gentlemanly effort."

He reached for the snap on her jeans.

"I can do that myself!"

"Darn."

"What about gentlemanly efforts?"

"In the last forty-eight hours I've used up my lifetime allotment of gentlemanly efforts. That was the last one I had left." He gave a distraught glance at the shape of her nipples poking against the maroon-and-yellow jersey. "The least you could do is be less . . . voluptuous."

Chris looked down at herself. "I can't help it. I'm cold." As if on cue, her teeth began to chatter and goose bumps erupted on her arms.

"You need to get into bed." In one swift movement he had her jeans unsnapped and down to her knees. He pulled one cuff and then the other and expertly rolled her under the covers.

"You're awfully good at removing ladies' Levi's. You must have had tons of practice."

"I practice every chance I get."

Chris let herself sink back into the pillow. She closed her eyes and allowed Ken to tuck the feather quilt under her chin. It was awful being sick, but it was very nice to be on the receiving end of such loving care. If Edna had been home she would have trundled her off to bed with a stern lecture about "taking care of oneself." And when Edna wasn't looking Lucy would have brought her freshly made crayon drawings and smuggled her treats from the kitchen. A sudden wave of loneliness for the little girl washed over Chris. She felt her eyes fill with tears.

Ken perched on the edge of the bed, studying her with a concerned face. "Tears? What's the matter?"

"I—I miss Lucy!" she sniffled. She wiped her eyes with the back of her hands. "Goodness, just look at me—I'm pathetic . . . lying here, crying for my daughter. I feel like such a boob."

Ken smiled and stroked her hair from her forehead. "You're not a boob. You're just sick, and you miss your family. Why don't we do something to take your mind off it." He reached out and took a paperback book from the night table. "When my little sisters were sick I used to read to them. Would you like me to read to you?"

Chris looked at the book he held in his hand. It was a romance. An engraved leather bookmark innocently rested between the pages of a torrid love scene. Ordinarily, she would never have been able to put the book down at such a spot, but an especially exhausting weekend had caused her to drop off to sleep even as the hero's hand crept up the heroine's thigh.

Aching bones and throbbing head were not sufficient to extinguish the humor of the situation. Chris could barely control the impulse to laugh out loud at the idea of Ken Callahan reading her love scenes while she had the plague. It was the ultimate practical joke. She was too sick to get aroused, and he was too nice to resort to rape. *Goodness,* she thought, *I'm an awful person. His offer to read to me is such a sweet gesture . . . and here I am snickering over the inevitable outcome.* She slid deeper under the covers, hoping to hide the horrible smile that kept creeping across her mouth. "Mmmm," she mumbled, "I'd like you to read to me."

He opened the book to the bookmark and scanned the page. Chris watched him closely, but his face remained impassive. He flipped back a few pages. "Would you mind if I started at the beginning of the chapter? I've never been any good at walking into the middle of a movie . . . or, in this case, starting in the middle of a chapter."

Chris gave silent assent. She closed her eyes in deference to the pounding headache and lay perfectly still, hoping to diminish the nausea. Ken read in a low, velvety voice that drifted soothingly through the fog of fever. The story was already familiar to her and required little concentration. She heard only a few disconnected sentences before falling into a restless sleep.

Chris opened her eyes to find sunlight splashing across her comforter. There was a moment of panic until she realized it was Saturday and she could oversleep legally. A memory of the preceding night sifted through the sluggish drowse. "Oh no. Oh darn." She groaned softly, attempting to rise to a sitting position. She propped herself up against the headboard and broke out into a cold sweat from the effort.

"Are you okay?"

Chris turned toward the familiar rumble of Ken's bedroom voice to find him slouched casually in the overstuffed club chair in the corner of her room. He half reclined in the chair with one sock-clad foot on the floor and one resting on the ottoman that matched the chair. His red plaid flannel shirt hung unbuttoned and untucked, giving silent testimony that he'd slept in his clothes; and, from the dark smudges under his eyes, Chris guessed that he'd slept very badly. He stood and stretched, unconsciously displaying an intriguing patch of dark hair under his shirt and a tantalizingly masculine bulge behind his zipper. Chris managed a weak smile and decided she must be feeling better. Really sick people didn't get that much pleasure just from ogling a bulge.

Ken sat at the edge of her bed and lay his hand against her cheek. "Glad to see you feeling better. You had me scared for a while there last night. You were really sick until about two-thirty, and then your fever broke."

"I don't remember."

"You kept calling for Bruce. Who the hell is Bruce?"

"Bruce was my dog when I was a little girl. We were inseparable. He was a huge, shaggy sheepdog that loped after me wherever I went. He died from old age when I was nine years old."

Ken looked disgusted. "You mean I spent the better part of the night being jealous of a dog?"

"Were you really jealous?"

"Um-hmmm." He covered her hand with his.

"I think I fell asleep while you were reading to me."

"You didn't even make it to the good part." He smiled roguishly. "That's some book. I always thought romances were for delicate, frail lady types. Do you know there are pages and pages of sex in that book?"

Chris bit back a smile. "Gee, I'm sorry I missed it."

"That's okay. I marked my favorite pages." His eyes sparkled dangerously. "When you're feeling better we can read them together."

"You marked your favorite pages?" She looked at the book lying on the floor beside the club chair. White strips of paper fluttered throughout. "You read the whole book."

He looked embarrassed. His swarthy complexion colored red under the black beard. "You were so sick . . . I was afraid to leave you alone, and it . . . uh . . . it gave me something to do." He stood up suddenly and plunged his hand into his pocket. "Well, hell," he grinned good-naturedly, "the truth is . . . I enjoyed it." His eyes raked across her nightshirt. They crinkled into laugh lines and his teeth flashed white in a dazzling smile of laughter turned inward. "You can't imagine how frustrating it was."

Chris wrinkled her nose and frowned. Didn't the man ever do anything rotten? How could she kick him out of her life when he was such a good sport about everything? How could anyone not love Ken Callahan? "Damn."

"Damn?"

She slumped into her pillow. "I practically snickered myself to sleep last night knowing you would be in a state when you got to all those juicy love scenes. And now instead of getting grumpy and testy, you have the nerve to be adorable about it."

"Adorable? Hmmm. I've never thought of myself as being adorable. Puppies and baby dresses and stuffed animals are adorable. Garfield is adorable." He straightened his spine. "I've always thought of myself more as . . . irresistible."

Chris responded with a heavy-lidded smile. *Yes,* she thought, *you're irresistible. But there are times when you're also adorable, and I find it every bit as incongruous as you do. It's amazing that anyone so masculine and so virile could have kept enough little-boy vulnerability to make him adorable.*

Ken straightened the comforter and tucked it in around Chris. "What's the verdict? Is this a case of major flu? Or is this one of those twenty-four-hour things?"

"I think it's just twenty-four-hour. I'm not nauseous, and I don't think I have a fever." She held her head with both hands. "Just residual headache."

"And from the white pallor of your otherwise glowing complexion I would guess you're pretty weak."

Chris sank lower into her pillow. "Nothing two or three days' worth of solid sleep wouldn't cure."

"Do you think you should see a doctor?"

"No!"

He nodded his head. "Okay. How about some tea and toast?"

"I'd rather have coffee and a waffle."

His eyebrow quirked over one eye in reprimand, and he sauntered from the room.

Sunday morning Chris swung her legs over the side of the bed and reveled in the glorious feeling of being healthy and rested. The aroma of freshly brewed coffee washed over her in warm, tantalizing waves. Her man was in the kitchen. *Her man.* The phrase almost knocked the wind out of her. She rose from the bed on shaky legs, knowing it wasn't flu that made her tremble—it was the anticipation of seeing Ken. For two days he'd brought her flowers and books and meals. He'd rolled the color TV into her room, and he'd gotten movies for the VCR.

He'd stayed with her, sharing her recuperation in a quiet, comfy way, sitting on the bed or in the club chair, and he kept an atmosphere of companionable silence, allowing her to doze and leaving time for her to think private thoughts—mostly of him. Mostly thoughts she had no business thinking. Thoughts about a man in her future. A man who would be a real father to Lucy, teaching her soccer and softball and grilling prospective suitors. A man Chris could talk to in the privacy of her bedroom. Not sexy talk—just regular talk, like "Vicki Jamison drove me nuts today," or "Orange juice was half-price at Super-Duper, so I bought twelve gallons."

It was easy to imagine Ken Callahan as such a man. He was the stuff dreams were made of—and she loved him. Lord, how she loved him. It was a bittersweet, lump-in-the-throat sort of love. It was a love she would have to guard closely and keep in her secret heart of hearts because fear of another betrayal knotted her stomach and fluttered wildly in her chest. It was irrational and ungrounded, she told herself, but it was real.

She padded to the top of the stairs and called down to Ken.

Instantly, he appeared at the bottom step with a wooden

spoon in his hand and a cookbook stuffed under his arm. This was going to be impossible, Chris thought, grinning. How could any woman resist this guy? She grasped hold of the stair rail to keep from flinging herself into his arms and struggled to assume a cheerful voice.

"Look at me. I'm actually a human being today."

"So I see," he murmured, his eyes full of lazy seduction. "And looking very good."

Ken Callahan was peeking up her nightie. She stumbled backward, feeling inexplicably shy. She waited for the rush of excitement to subside in her stomach before speaking. "What are you making?"

"It was supposed to be a surprise. I was going to bring you breakfast in bed."

"No!" Yesterday he'd made rubber Jell-O that couldn't be cut with a steak knife. He had permanently fused two inches of cooked, congealed, totally burned oatmeal to the bottom of her best saucepan. And he had cooked a pot roast for three hours before discovering it was wrapped in cellophane.

His face grew quizzical at her adamant "no."

"I'm feeling better—I'll make breakfast this morning," she insisted. "Give me a minute to shower, and I'll be right down."

He looked relieved. "That sounds nice. To tell you the truth I was a little nervous about trying to make waffles on my own. Sometimes my first attempts at new recipes don't turn out so well."

Chris turned before he could see the look of incredulity on her face. Sometimes his first attempts didn't turn out so well—what an understatement!

She stripped and jumped into the steaming shower. Five minutes later she was tripping down the stairs in a pair of snug jeans and a white T-shirt that sported a glittery picture of Daffy Duck. Her still-damp hair curled in little ringlets around her face. A slash of lavender shadow and clear lip gloss were her only concessions to makeup. By the time she cleared the last step her heart was skipping beats over the knowledge that she'd purposely neglected to wear a bra under the flimsy T-shirt. The dusky hint of nipples was not hidden by Daffy Duck, and the jiggle and sway of loose breasts was enticement and she wasn't sure why she was doing it. She was asking for trouble and enjoying every minute of it.

Ken lounged against a kitchen counter and watched her approach. A small tight smile quirked at his mouth, and his eyes darkened under heavy black lashes. "Hmmmm," was his only comment, uttered in a low velvet growl.

Chris experienced a moment of searing panic. She had forgotten how fast he could change from adorable puppy to awesome predator. She spread her arms wide and resumed the role of forced gaiety to hide her confusion. "Well, here I am. Ready to make you a great breakfast. What would you like to eat?"

His eyes burned a path from her mouth to her protruding nipples. "What's on the menu?"

"Waffles?" she asked hopefully, swallowing hard.

"Is that the best you can do?"

"Ah-h-h-h," she quavered. "Oh, shoot." Chris stomped across the kitchen, hands on hips, eyes narrowed. "What is it about you that scares the heck out of me? I walked down those stairs filled with confidence and feeling seductive . . . and all you have to do is look at me and drop your voice an octave and I'm . . . I'm . . ."

"Mush?"

"Mush."

Ken tipped his head back and laughed softly. "I don't think there's another woman alive that would come right out and say something like that." He reached out and pulled her into the circle of his arms. He watched her for a few seconds before drawing her closer. "I don't want you to be afraid of what you feel for me. We have a special attraction for each other. It should be enjoyed and cherished." He lowered his lips to hers and kissed her tenderly. "If we take care of this attraction it will grow even stronger, and it will last a long, long time. It's not just hormones, Chris. It's a union of minds and hearts and secret dreams." His cast rested against her hipbone. His right hand flattened over her back, pushing her against him, crushing her breasts into his hard, muscled chest. "Lean on me, Chris," he coaxed. "Daffy Duck won't mind."

Chris felt the smile creep through her. It tickled her fingertips and surged through her heart. She did as he asked and leaned into him, her thighs sliding suggestively between his, her stomach flat against the snap of his Levi's.

He shifted his weight to fit her even more snugly to him and whispered her name in a voice thickened by emotion. His hand impatiently roamed across her back in sensual exploration. It slid to her waist with increasing pressure. Finally, cupping her buttocks, he pressed her pelvic bone into his hardened manhood. "Oh Lord, Chris, I need you so bad. I want to feel you against every part of me."

She felt the heat rip through her as his arousal nudged into her stomach. Her nipples became sizzling nubs jutting demandingly into Ken's unyielding chest as liquid fire burned under her white lace bikini panties. She moaned at the rush that tumbled her stomach and parted her lips in longing expectation.

"I want to love you." His voice was barely audible.

Chris wrapped her arms around him. She kissed the spot on his neck where a few black hairs curled from the open V of his blue buttoned-down shirt. Her panic was gone. It was replaced with a pleasure so intense it bordered on pain. When he held her like this everything was right in the world. They belonged together, and she realized that this moment of affirmation had been as inevitable as April rain. "I want to love you, too," she whispered as she kissed the pulse point just below his jaw, touching it first with her lips and then with the tip of her tongue.

A gasp escaped from deep in Ken's throat at the erotic gesture. In an instant his mouth was on hers. The tentative gentleness of his previous kisses was gone, yielding to the overpowering passion that tore through both of them. Chris opened her mouth to the hard thrust of his tongue and rocked her hips against him in an invitation evocative of the rhythm that would eventually join them as one entity. She felt her shirt fall to the floor and looked down in wonderment at her own bare swollen breast resting in Ken's large dark hand. He began a maddeningly slow exploratory massage around the dark aureola. He rubbed the engorged nipple between his thumb and forefinger, and Chris gave herself up to the black all-encompassing desire that she had hoped to avoid.

He was right. It was special, and it was to be enjoyed and nurtured. She took his hand and led him upstairs to her bedroom, relishing her newfound bravery. "Look at what a bold hussy I've turned into," she laughed as she sprawled onto her apricot bed.

He covered her with his hard, seeking body, raining hot, urgent kisses across her face and down her throat while he whispered his approval. His shirt had been discarded somewhere between kitchen and bedroom, and his hair-rough chest burned over the reddened, sensitized peaks that crowned her soft high breasts. She arched against him, oblivious of everything but the need to love him fiercely and to quench the fire that raged within her. Their remaining clothes were quickly discarded, and his mouth closed hungrily over her nipple as she struggled to touch every part of him. She wanted to memorize the contour of his spine. To feel the excited nub of his small hard male nipple. To tangle her fingers in the thick black triangle of hair that was finally enticingly exposed. She watched his eyes blacken as she ran her palm along the smooth taut skin of his straining arousal.

"Chris!" The word was spoken softly but with enough authority to make her pay attention. He paused a moment, collecting himself. He positioned himself above her and kissed the moist skin between her breasts. His lips and tongue moved lower, slowly ravaging the length of her until they reached the tangle of light brown curls and found the most delicate, sensitive spot on her body. Convulsions of exquisite pleasure radiated in numbing waves from that perfect spot until Chris thought she could bear no more. "Now," she whispered, pulling him over her, guiding him between her trembling legs.

She closed her eyes, reveling in the sweetness of the first thrust that symbolized union to her . . . in every possible way. And then she was lost in the rhythm, crying out again as his own efforts toward release tugged at her tender, swollen flesh and dragged her back into the vortex of desire. Their bodies responded as one, pausing at the pinnacle, their eyes meeting for a split second to reveal the desperate naked need they felt for each other. The cords of his neck strained as he plunged into her and they pulsed together in loving release.

Chris listened in awe to the beating of his heart. His sweat-slicked body shuddered slightly at the effort of withdrawal, as if he couldn't bear to be separated from her. He rolled to his side and pulled her close, cradling her in the crook of his shoulder, positioning her so that he could feel the weight of her body against him. Chris pressed her face into his chest to hide the tears that were gathering in her eyes. She was overwhelmed with emotion, with love that was so strong it squeezed the air from her lungs.

When his breathing had slowed to normal he kissed her forehead. "I'm sorry, Chris."

She tipped her head toward his face. "What are you sorry for?"

"I wanted this to be perfect. I wanted to go slow the first time, but I think I lost control." He pulled back a bit to look at her. "I guess I make love like I cook. The first time I do it I never get it quite right."

"You mean it gets better than that?"

He grinned devilishly and shifted his weight. She felt something hard stir between her legs. "Lady, you ain't seen nothing, yet!"

Chapter Seven

CHRIS WATCHED THE patterns of moonlight on her bedroom wall and listened to the even breathing of the man next to her. It was odd to suddenly share her bed like this. There had been so few nights of her life spent in the company of a lover. She tried to dredge up memories of nights spent with Steven, but found there were none. Her whole being was filled with the present . . . with Ken. No more ghosts, she thought happily. And no more panicky fears of rejection and betrayal. She loved him, and she didn't want to hold anything back from him. All the walls she had so carefully and painfully built would have to be destroyed. Her heart told her she could trust him, and she believed her heart. It was a lovely luxury. Vulnerability is vastly underestimated, she thought dreamily. You don't fully appreciate it until you've denied it to yourself for a long time.

She turned from the moonlight shadows to study his sleeping silhouette. Even in sleep, there was a strength to his face and a protective tension in his body that made her feel safe and cosseted. It would be nice to be married to this man, she decided. He made her bed comfy. And he was nice to love. Gentle and fierce and honest. She felt overwhelmed at the memory of their lovemaking. She had never shared herself so fully with a man. She pressed her cheek against his bare shoulder and enjoyed the faint aroma